"YOU'RE NOT REALLY SCARED OF ME," MATT WHISPERED.

Kate struggled weakly in his arms. "I am!" she objected unconvincingly.

"I can hear your heart beating, feel your skin warm to my touch. You're not scared, Kate, you're excited."

His embrace had her nearly breathless. "Stop," she whispered, though a fire had started to burn within her. "Please, Matt . . . Do you think you can just do whatever you want with me?"

"You know I can," he replied softly. "And deep down, you want me to, don't you? Try to deny it, Kate. I dare you. Whatever I have to do to unlock all the passion I know you're capable of, I'll do. And there won't be a thing you can do to stop me."

CANDLELIGHT SUPREMES

141 WINDS OF A SECRET DESIRE, *Deborah Sherwood*
142 MYSTERY IN THE MOONLIGHT, *Lynn Patrick*
143 ENDLESS OBSESSION, *Hayton Monteith*
144 MY DARLING PRETENDER, *Linda Vail*
145 UNDERCOVER AFFAIR, *Sydney Ann Clary*
146 THE WANDERER'S PROMISE, *Paula Hamilton*
147 LAYING DOWN THE LAW, *Donna Kimel Vitek*
148 ROMAN FANTASY, *Betty Henrichs*
149 TODAY AND ALWAYS, *Alison Tyler*
150 THE NIGHT OF HIS LIFE, *Blair Cameron*
151 MURPHY'S CHARM, *Linda Randall Wisdom*
152 IN THE HEAT OF THE SUN, *Anne Silverlock*
153 JEWEL OF INDIA, *Sue Gross*
154 BREATHLESS TEMPTATION, *Eleanor Woods*
155 A MAN TO REMEMBER, *Tate McKenna*
156 DANGER IN PARADISE, *Kit Daley*

SHATTERED SECRETS

Linda Vail

A CANDLELIGHT SUPREME

Published by
Dell Publishing Co., Inc.
1 Dag Hammarskjold Plaza
New York, New York 10017

ISBN: 0-440-17983-1

Printed in the United States of America

February 1987

10 9 8 7 6 5 4 3 2 1

WFH

To Our Readers:

We are pleased and excited by your overwhelmingly positive response to our Candlelight Supremes. Unlike all the other series, the Supremes are filled with more passion, adventure, and intrigue, and are obviously the stories you like best.

In months to come we will continue to publish books by many of your favorite authors as well as the very finest work from new authors of romantic fiction. As always, we are striving to present unique, absorbing love stories —the very best love has to offer.

Breathtaking and unforgettable, Supremes follow in the great romantic tradition you've come to expect *only* from Candlelight Romances.

Your suggestions and comments are always welcome. Please let us hear from you.

Sincerely,

The Editors
Candlelight Romances
1 Dag Hammarskjold Plaza
New York, New York 10017

SHATTERED SECRETS

CHAPTER ONE

"Have I actually managed to stumble upon the only single woman here, or did you just forget to wear your wedding ring this evening?"

Kate Asher almost dropped her plate when she turned toward the man who slipped into the buffet line beside her. He was at least six three, with a powerfully muscular build even his impeccably tailored navy blue suit couldn't disguise. His shoulders were broad, his chest deep, tapering to what looked to be a flat stomach and lean hips.

A tad over five six herself, Kate still had to tilt her head slightly to look at the big man's deeply tanned face. He was smiling, showing a healthy array of even, white teeth. There were laugh lines around his mouth and at the corners of his eyes, eyes the color of emerald ice. His sandy blond hair was longish and sleekly styled.

"I'm Matthew Gage," the man told her in a deep, pleasant voice.

"Kate Asher." She shook his hand, disturbed by the alarming way her heartbeat quickened at the brief touch.

"Pleased to meet you, Kate." Was he ever,

Matt thought, noting her shoulder-length auburn hair, robin's egg blue eyes, and trim, athletic body outlined beneath her soft peach-colored knee-length dress of some tantalizingly thin material. "Why don't we sneak out of here and go someplace nice and quiet, maybe have a drink and get to know each other better?" he asked, leaning closer so only she could hear his soft invitation.

Kate looked at him, her eyes wide, trying to ignore the way his hip kept brushing against hers as they moved along. "Aren't you enjoying the banquet, Mr. Gage?"

He chuckled, a resonant sound she could feel as well as hear. "I wasn't," he replied, his eyes sparkling as they slowly roved over her well-rounded curves again, "until I met you. And call me Matt. All my friends do."

From the way his gaze lingered covetously on her breasts, Kate had little doubt he intended to become as friendly as he could as fast as he could. Though she couldn't deny feeling attracted to him as well, tonight of all nights she could ill afford to be the object of anyone's attention—as flattering as that attention might be. Then, too, there was something hard about Matthew Gage; he seemed capable and vaguely frightening.

"You were right before," she informed him as she turned her gaze back to the attractively arranged buffet table. "I did forget to wear my wedding ring this evening."

"Oh."

It wasn't entirely a lie. She was still Mrs.

Asher, but her husband had died two years before in an auto accident. And she did wear her wedding band on occasion, though she had recently decided to put that last remnant of the past aside and was having it made into a stylish dinner ring.

Kate noticed his humorously crestfallen expression and served him an extra helping of strawberry mousse. "Single women are few and far between at insurance company banquets, Matt," she told him.

"So I've noticed," he said forlornly. "I guess I'll just have to make do with the free food."

She knew how he felt. For a single man or woman on the prowl, these affairs held slim pickings. The president of Fidelity Insurance, the company her husband had worked for as an insurance investigator, still invited her to the monthly soirees. It was courteous and typical of their loyal familylike company image, but Kate rarely accepted. Though she had a few friends here, she felt like the odd one out among all the married couples now that her husband was gone.

Leaving the buffet to find a quiet corner, Kate was surprised to see Matthew Gage following her. Why wasn't he going off to hunt other, more encouraging game? She hid a secretive smile at the way he sat down across from her and made an elaborate display of concentrating on his food. Either he didn't believe her wedding ring story or it didn't make any difference to him. Kate found his persistence annoying and exciting at the same time.

Was there really any reason to burn her bridges

behind her? She may not want him hanging around tonight, but she was much too aware of his masculine interest and its thrilling effect on her to want him to get lost permanently. Maybe she could tell him the truth, see what he had in mind, then give him the slip later when it came time to go on the fact-finding mission that had brought her there.

"I take it you haven't been with the company long, Matt?"

He looked up from his dinner and gazed at her speculatively. "You might say this is my first day," he replied. "You?"

"I . . . Actually, I don't work here at all," she told him honestly. As interested in her as he seemed, he'd probably find out from somebody else anyway. "My late husband did."

Matt's eyebrows arched. "Late husband?"

"Paul was with the company ten years at the time of his death and had a lot of friends here. They're my friends, too, so I guess you could say I'm still a part of the Fidelity family."

"That explains it," Matt mumbled. "I thought I was losing my touch."

"Excuse me?"

He pointed to her left hand. "You have a nice tan and no white mark where your wedding ring would be. When you said you'd forgotten to wear it, I figured you were trying to get rid of me."

"Observant, aren't you?" Kate asked dryly.

Matt shrugged. "It depends on what I'm observing," he replied. There was a definite power in his icy green eyes, and he was using it right now as he gazed at her intently. "Right now, for instance, I'm observing a very sexy woman who can't seem to decide what to do about me. That makes you a challenge, Kate Asher, and I plan to keep a close watch on you all evening."

"Oh, really?" she returned, forcing a casual smile in spite of the disturbing fluttering in her stomach. If he meant what he said he could spoil everything. She had to get away from him somehow.

"Really."

"What if I told you to get lost?"

Matt grinned. "I'd just think you were confused. After all, something made you change your mind and tell me the truth about your marital status."

"At first I thought I liked the way you didn't give up right away," she explained. "But I'm beginning to find your perseverance a bit grating, Mr. Gage."

"That's me. Persistent." He reached across the table and touched her hand, his eyes never leaving her face. "I've got a lot of stamina, too. Is that a quality you like as well, Kate?" he asked, his thumb gently rubbing the inside of her wrist.

How had she gotten herself into this situation? she wondered. A man she didn't know at all was making her entire body tingle with his touch and the look in his eyes, while talking about stamina of all things! And she knew he wasn't referring to his ability to run races or lift weights.

Though she wasn't immune to the thrill of his touch, or the equally disturbing images his innuendo brought flooding into her mind, Kate decided she had to cool him off—and fast.

"Oh, I don't know, Matt," she said as calmly as she could. "Anybody who moves as quickly as you do couldn't possibly last long enough to suit me."

His eyes wide, Matt laughed so hard he shook the table they shared, drawing more than a few interested glances in his direction. He didn't seem to notice or care, but Kate did. She wanted to blend into the woodwork tonight, and this wasn't the way to go about it at all.

"We'll have to get together sometime, Kate," he said in a smooth tone, "so I can show you just how long I can last."

Kate cleared her throat and started to stand up. "I think I've had about as much of you as I can take already."

"I doubt that." His hand clasped her arm, easily preventing her from slipping away. "You look strong to me, Kate Asher. Fine muscle tone, beautiful long legs. I think you and I are going to have a perfectly delicious time trying to figure out which of us is tougher."

She'd been right. He was a threat to her mission; he was powerful and outrageously self-confident. "Tell you what, Mr. Gage," she replied, her voice frosty. "Why don't you just start without me? You seem to love yourself enough to barely notice I'm gone."

Matt chuckled and released her arm from his grasp. "I'm not snubbed that easily," he informed her calmly as she turned to leave. "I'm persistent, remember?"

"That you are, Mr. Gage." She glared at him. "A very persistent pain." With that she sauntered off to seek refuge in the ladies' room, her heart thumping in her chest.

It took her quite some time to calm down. She had been nervous enough about her clandestine plans for this evening without the added worry of fending off the advances of a man who refused to take no for an answer.

When she emerged from the lounge a while later and looked around tentatively, Kate breathed a sigh of relief—she didn't see Matthew Gage anywhere. In spite of his brash, openly sexual manner, however, she found herself almost hoping she hadn't seen the last of him. But there wasn't time for her to ask herself why. The monthly lecture was about to start, and people were filtering out of the company cafeteria to head for the main conference room.

Kate walked with them, trying to blend in with the crowd and avoid anyone who might grab her and escort her to the lecture. The last thing she wanted was to be seen sneaking out later.

At the doorway to the conference room she paused, making a show of digging in her purse and muttering to herself. She must have been convincing, because when she turned and went back toward the cafeteria no one gave her a second glance. A quick left turn at the end of the corridor put her out of the reach of prying eyes, and another brought her to the elevators.

"Come on," she muttered, jabbing the up button several times, feeling exposed and vulnerable.

Though the corridor was empty, she imagined a thousand eyes were upon her, watching her every move. Tension crawling along her nerve endings like an electrical charge, she practically dove into the relative safety of the elevator when it arrived, holding her breath until the doors closed. The unseen cable above her head lifted her up and away, pressing her feet against the floor and adding yet another giant butterfly to her already queasy stomach.

No one had seen her. Nor did any authoritative voices call out for her to stop when she arrived at the tenth floor and made her way down yet another blessedly empty hallway. She forced herself to breathe deeply, telling herself this was necessary. If she didn't search for the truth no one would. It was now or never, and she had come much too far to turn back.

It had been quite some time since Kate had been in this part of the building, but the layout hadn't changed and she quickly found the department where the mountains of insurance case files and field reports were rendered onto computer disks. Now came the tricky part.

If company routine was running true to form, the keypunch people in records would have come on at six and taken a break to go to the banquet; they would return to finish their shift as soon as the lecture was over.

Creeping to the door, she peeked through the small eye-level window and saw no activity. She crossed her fingers and tried the door. It was unlocked. Taking a deep breath, she stepped inside, fully prepared to find herself face to face with a security guard. But the room was empty, a placid whirring noise from the computers the only sound.

Kate was frightened out of her wits, but felt surprisingly little guilt as she took a seat at one of the terminals and began going through the files. Except for the fear of getting caught it was like old times, really. She had worked in this department when she had met her late husband. Though the policy had since been changed, at the time husbands and wives couldn't both work for the company, so when they had married, Kate had quit, fully intent on becoming a happy housewife.

Three short years later, Paul had died in a fiery one-car accident on a deserted stretch of highway between Phoenix and Tucson. In addition to the devastation of losing him, Kate had been overwhelmed with suspicion.

Hardly James Bond, Paul had still been an investigator, reviewing claims where millions of dollars balanced on his detective work and settlement adjustments. And he had been an excellent, cautious driver, not even a traffic ticket on his record. She had voiced those facts and her suspicions loudly at the time, had made herself something of a nuisance, actually, particularly in the eyes of Fidelity.

But both the police and the company ruled her husband's death an accident, plain and simple.

Her protests fell on increasingly deaf ears as the months rolled by. Paul had left her well provided for—naturally, since he worked for an insurance firm—and as frequently happened with the passage of time, Kate's suspicions had eventually subsided along with her grief.

Until a month ago.

It had been like going through it all again. This time it was a friend of hers who lost her husband in a senseless accident. David Tynly was a Fidelity insurance investigator too, and the circumstances of his death—though ruled accidental—seemed mysterious. A powerful swimmer who had come within a few tenths of a second of earning a place on America's Olympic team, Gloria's husband had drowned in the midst of looking into another unusually large life insurance claim.

As she helped Gloria through her bereavement, something inside Kate snapped. She had had enough of coincidences, of being told that accidents happened, more than her fill of Fidelity's sympathetic yet vaguely patronizing assurances.

Now she felt precious little remorse at this highly unauthorized perusal of the company's files. The Fidelity people were hiding something, she was sure of it, and since they were intent on stonewalling her, she was just as intent on discovering the truth. She viewed this not as breaking the law but as a debt she owed to Paul.

"Tell me, Mr. President," Kate muttered vindictively as she peered at the computer monitor, "if you find nothing suspicious about the claims

Paul was investigating when he died, why the sudden interest in his old case files?"

When she cross-referenced those with the claims David Tynly had been working on, she found the same recent requests for hard copies. Even more interesting was her discovery that all information pertaining to the files in question had been shifted to another level of the records program. A one-line description of the file contents, its number, and activity dates were as much as she could get without an access code.

Deciding to risk the noise, she tried to defeat the program by sneaking in the back way, punching in the numbers of the files she wanted to read and requesting printouts. The message REQUIRES PROPER AUTHORIZATION appeared on the terminal screen.

"I hope all your circuits burn out!" Kate told the machine viciously.

There were other ways. Dale Johnson, president of Fidelity Insurance, had an office on the top floor of the building. He would be at the lecture, presenting monthly awards, and his office would be empty. It would still be risky, and she might run into a security guard, but Kate felt certain she would find the files she was looking for in Dale's office. Besides, if anyone caught her, she would just pretend to be a banquet guest who had lost her way while looking around.

Kate made her way back to the elevators, rode to the top floor, and came within a few inches of getting the opportunity to try out her excuse for being there. When the elevator stopped and the doors slid open, a burly security guard stood directly in front of her.

At first he looked surprised. Then his eyes narrowed slightly and he opened his mouth. "Excuse me, ma'am, but what are you—"

"Oops!" Kate interrupted, hoping the terror she felt would look like embarrassment. "I pushed the wrong button."

With a trembling hand she reached out and pushed another button on the panel, then smiled weakly under the guard's suspicious gaze during the eternity it took for the elevator doors to close. When they finally did close she had to grab the brass railing at her side to keep from crumpling to the floor of the car.

"Oh, Lord," she moaned. "Now what?"

The elevator lurched to a stop and she held her breath, but this time no one was waiting outside the door. Suddenly realizing that the guard would be watching to see what floor the car stopped on next, she jabbed the button for the parking level and jumped out into the hall, hoping he would think she had just made another mistake.

There was no way around it now. She would have to use the stairs. Kate was in good shape, and normally the three flights of steps wouldn't have bothered her at all. As it was, though, scared of every sound and practically afraid to breathe, she arrived back at the top floor panting, her pulse so quick she could feel it beating in her throat.

She could see the headline now: *Kate Asher*

FOUND DEAD OF HEART FAILURE ON STAIRS OF FIDELITY BUILDING.

Leaning against the wall of the stairwell, Kate waited until the adrenaline level in her bloodstream dropped back to something approaching normal before opening the fire door and peeking out. She could see the elevators, as well as the guard, who was still looking at the floor indicator and scratching his chin. His back was to her.

Kate slipped out into the hall, carefully making sure the door made no sound as it closed behind her, then tiptoed down the corridor and away from the security man. Her breathing, still labored with fright from the close call she'd had, sounded so loud to her she was sure the whole building could hear. But she made it to the president's office without seeing another soul.

She put her hand on the doorknob, a sinking feeling deep within her telling her it would be locked. She tried it anyway. When the knob turned without a hitch she arched her eyebrows in surprise.

What if Dale Johnson was in there, or another guard, or even a cleaning person? Kate decided she had to risk it. It would be better to go down in flames than get caught standing there like a dummy. Alert to any sound, she tentatively pushed the door open.

And walked straight into the strong, unyielding arms of Matthew Gage.

CHAPTER TWO

"Looking for someone?"

Kate gasped.

"Me perhaps?" Matt grinned and pulled her the rest of the way into the office, closing the door behind her and putting one of his big hands on either side of her shoulders, trapping her between his arms. "I had the feeling you'd reconsider my offer," he said, his voice barely above a whisper. "You were just playing hard to get, right?"

"What the hell are you doing here?" Kate demanded.

"Bold question coming from a woman who prowls around a building several floors above where she's supposed to be," he replied with a chuckle. "But I had you pegged for a bold woman the moment I saw you." Matt leaned still closer, his chest resting intimately against hers. He could feel the heat of her body mix with his and grinned as she pressed herself against the office door, away from his touch. "Answer my question. Were you looking for me?"

Kate could feel his breath on her cheek and

was intensely aware of his size and strength so close to her. Barely an inch separated them now and she struggled to prevent her body from betraying her feelings, surprised by the way all her senses seemed to come alive at his nearness. She could still feel the imprint of his chest against hers.

"No! I was . . ." She searched her mind for an explanation. "I was looking for Mr. Johnson. We—"

The big man sighed forlornly. "Please, please don't tell me you two have a thing going. I couldn't bear the thought of taking a woman away from a nice guy like Dale."

"We most certainly do not!" Kate cried in outrage. "Who do you think you are to accost me like this, threaten me and—"

Matt thrust his body against hers, every conceivable inch of his strength weighing on her as he flattened her against the door. His hips pressed firmly into hers as he grabbed and held her hands captive over her head.

"I haven't even begun to accost you," he whispered, nipping the delicate skin on her neck.

"Stop . . ." Her voice trailed off, replaced by soft gasps for breath as his lips traced the curve of her jaw and slipped lower, along the line of her throat. "How dare you even—"

"Oh, I dare," he taunted softly. His lips rose back along her throat, stopping to nuzzle her earlobe.

Kate closed her eyes against the simmering emotions coursing through her. It had been a long time since she'd felt this way. She swayed toward him involuntarily.

Suddenly his head came up and stared boldly into her eyes. "Threaten you?" Matt pushed away from her, giving her back her freedom. "All I said was that if you're Dale's woman, you won't be for long," he replied, smiling placidly. "That's not a threat, Kate." He winked. "That's a promise."

Fists clenched at her sides, Kate blew out the breath she had been holding in a disbelieving sigh. "Now I see why you're so tall, Mr. Gage. You need the height to hold all that ego!" Damn the man anyway! He could have at least kissed her while he was at it and satisfied her curiosity.

What was she thinking? "You must be crazy!" she cried in outrage, mad at herself as well as him.

"Doubting my capability, Kate?"

No, she wasn't. That was the trouble. He looked and acted like a very capable man. She didn't doubt for a moment that his overwhelming self-confidence came from knowing his own abilities. He frightened her, and the knowledge that he would be relentless in his pursuit of her frightened her even more. It also made her nerve endings tingle for a reason she couldn't explain.

"I think you're too capable for your own good, Mr. Gage," Kate replied with more bravado than she felt. "Now you answer my question. What are you doing here? Where's Dale?"

Matt crossed his arms over his broad chest, his expression full of patient amusement. He glanced at his watch. "Fidelity's beloved president is in the lecture hall congratulating the employee of the month about now, I imagine. But I'm sure you're well aware of that or you wouldn't be here, would you? As for what I'm doing here, well, I'd say that isn't any of your business."

"Suits me." Kate turned and put her hand on the doorknob, anxious to get away from this man and the disturbing feelings he had awakened within her. "I'll just be running along, then."

"Going back to the records department to have another go at the computer?" he asked when she was halfway out the door.

Kate stopped in her tracks, turned, and looked at him with what she hoped was a confused expression. "Excuse me?"

He stood there, gazing back at her speculatively, his lips drawn into a curiously evil smile. "The terminal in this office can display the activity taking place on any other terminal in the building. I was aware of your pathetic attempts to break into the files the moment you touched the keyboard down there," he explained in a patronizing tone. "You're out of your league, Mrs. Asher. Don't you know that? Just because your husband was a capable investigator doesn't make you one."

Kate's eyes widened. A short while ago he hadn't even known about her husband—or had pretended he didn't. Now he seemed to know a great deal, including what she'd been up to for the last half hour.

"I—I don't understand."

"Close the door," Matt ordered curtly, turning his back on her and crossing the office to Dale Johnson's massive oak desk.

Kate looked at the desk, saw that he had obviously been doing some kind of research, and felt constricting panic grip her heart. "What do you want?"

"A more appropriate question, Kate, is what do *you* want?" He took a seat at the desk, leaning back and lacing his fingers behind his head. "Sit down," he said, indicating the chair in front of the desk with a casual motion of his strong, angular jaw. "Unless you'd rather I call security. I'm sure they'd just love to find out somebody's been tiptoeing around them all evening."

Kate closed the door and did as he asked, glaring at him defiantly. "You were spying on me! What right—"

"I work here," he interrupted, "or at least in a manner of speaking I am employed by Fidelity. You're not. Haven't been for a number of years. What right do you have to try to gain access to company records?"

"How do you know so much about me and Paul?" she countered suspiciously.

Matt leaned forward, his eyes narrowing. "Answer the question, Mrs. Asher. What right do you have to be up here prowling around?"

"I have every right!" Kate's panic at being confronted with her transgression was rapidly turning to indignant outrage. "My late husband devoted a good part of his life to this company. He may have *lost* his life for this damn company. I have every right to get some answers and I'll get them any way I can."

Matt pursed his lips. "The official line on this matter is that Paul Asher died in an automobile accident on his way back from investigating a large but routine life insurance claim in Tucson," he said, his voice surprisingly soft. "The key word, Kate, is accident. The police thought so, the medical examiner thought so, and the adjuster who reviewed your own claim on your husband's policy thought so." He stood up and walked over to sit on the edge of the desk nearest her. "Why don't you think so?"

Although his manner had suddenly turned gentle and there was a certain amount of sympathy in his voice, his gaze remained hard and unwavering. Kate sensed this was a ploy, an attempt to get her to trust him. His insincerity made her angrier.

"I've had it up to here with the official story," she replied with disgust, drawing an imaginary line across her throat with a trembling hand. "And I'm sick of being treated as if I'm a grief-crazed widow with paranoid delusions." She glared at Matt, tears of frustration beginning to shimmer in her eyes. "I loved my husband, Mr. Gage, but he's gone. I accepted that long ago."

"Did you love him, Kate?"

She straightened in her chair. "What's that supposed to mean?"

"Dale told me Paul's death came during a rocky spot in your marriage," he replied. "Maybe you feel that if he hadn't died you could have worked things out, so you see the accident as something more suspicious because it robbed you of that chance."

"Spare me the pop psychology," she said derisively.

"You have to have some reason for being such a thorn in Fidelity's side." He shrugged. "And I have to start somewhere. I just want to know if you've considered the possibility that these doubts you have about the accident may be caused by your own feelings of guilt at not getting along with Paul just before he died."

Kate turned her face away from him, struggling not to let the tears in her eyes overflow to her cheeks. Of course she had asked herself that question, over and over since the accident. And maybe there were some feelings of guilt that the last thing she and Paul had done together was fight.

But she had learned to deal with those feelings, or at least had convinced herself she had. Besides, whoever this Matthew Gage was and no matter how concerned he pretended to be, he had no right to probe her emotions.

"If, as you say, you have to start somewhere, start with this," Kate told him, impatiently brushing her tears away and turning back to face him. "I'm not grieving, nor am I overcome with guilt. I'm mad, furious that no one is even bothering to listen to me."

"I'm listening," Matt said quietly.

"I don't need your sympathy, Mr. Gage."

He put his hand on her shoulder, his touch

light and dangerously reassuring. Was this yet another ploy? Kate looked into his eyes, taken aback by the understanding she saw there.

This was a man who refused to be taken lightly, one who seemed just as capable of tenderness as he was so obviously endowed with physical strength. Either his concern was genuine or he was a very good actor. She shivered involuntarily.

"We all need sympathy from time to time, Kate," he told her, his voice soft and coaxing. "If I were you I wouldn't be so anxious to push mine away."

Feeling a disturbing warmth wash over her, Kate stared at him, her mind and body in turmoil. In a voice scarcely above a whisper she asked, "Who are you, Mr. Gage?"

"I'm the man who is going to strangle you if you don't start calling me Matt," he replied, giving her shoulder a gentle, reproachful shake. "Or at the very least Matthew."

He stood up and returned to his seat behind the desk. She was too appealing and much too vulnerable at the moment for him to remain so close to her. A lot of questions had to be answered before Matt could allow himself to think about the excitement she evoked within him.

"Dale tells me you've been blissfully quiet about all this for quite a while," he continued after a moment of thoughtful silence. "No offense, Kate, but haven't you waited an awfully long time to carry your—um—investigation into your late husband's accident to these lengths?"

He waved his hand to indicate her unauthorized presence in that part of the building.

Kate's eyebrows arched in surprise. He really was listening to her, seemed to be honestly interested in what she was doing there rather than simply calling Dale and tossing her out on her ear.

Who was this man?

"You seem to be so well informed about all this, I'm sure you know the answer to that question." She peered at him accusingly. "That's why you're here, isn't it? To look into the untimely demise of David Tynly?"

He just stared at her, looking as if some piece of the puzzle had slipped into place for him. "I see. Gloria Tynly. I suppose you found her husband's accident suspicious too, finding enough similarities between it and Paul's to bring your theories about some kind of conspiracy to a boil again?"

Yes, he was well informed all right, and Kate wanted to know why. "I admit I had almost managed to put my suspicions behind me until a month ago," she replied, looking at him intently. "And I'm not the only one, am I? I couldn't get much out of the computer, but I got enough to prove there's been a sudden resurgence of interest in Paul's old case files. It's because of Gloria's husband's so-called accident, isn't it?"

"Why ask me?"

"Because you're part of this renewed interest."

"Am I?"

Kate stood up and leaned on the desk, fixing

him with a glare sharp enough to cut paper. "If you're not, why are we having this discussion, Matt?"

"Technically we're not," he replied just as curtly. "You're not even supposed to be here and I'm not supposed to be discussing anything with anybody."

"But I am here and you are talking to me, Matt." If he could change his demeanor from soft to hard at the drop of a hat, so could she. "Maybe I can help," she continued, smiling sweetly. "After all, I've been thinking about these odd coincidences a lot longer than you have."

His face placid, he gazed at her for a moment. "You're bold all right. Tough too." He chuckled heartily. "And maybe," he added, shaking his finger at her, "maybe just a little too smart. When I told you you were out of your league, Kate, I wasn't kidding."

"Then there is an official investigation?" she asked, triumph creeping into her voice.

"More like a discreet inquiry. And you're not listening to me. Dale asked me here tonight to brief me on this matter, and I admit I've only just started doing the research." He indicated the files strewn across the desk top. "But there do seem to be some odd things going on. If there's more than coincidence linking them together, it's bound to lead to something far more dangerous than a moonlight stroll through a nearly deserted insurance building."

"So you do believe me?"

Matt sighed and rubbed his face with his

hands. "Kate, it's my job to conduct an objective inquiry." He looked up at her. "I don't believe you, Dale, or anybody else. When I do believe something, it will be because I can prove it beyond a shadow of a doubt." He fixed her with a hard, penetrating glare and added sternly, "And I'll do it without any further interference from you. Is that clear?"

"No, it is not clear!" she exclaimed. "I have every right—"

"The only reason I'm talking to you is that, unlike Dale, I think you deserve to know something is being done to check out your suspicions." He grinned and eyed the way the neckline of her dress dipped fetchingly as she leaned across the desk. The fleeting taste of her smooth skin earlier had left him wanting even more of her. "That, and the fact that I have designs on your body."

Kate straightened abruptly and folded her arms over her chest. "Is that so?" she asked icily.

"Yes, Kate, that is most definitely so." He stood up and walked over to the office door, opened it, and looked at her pointedly. "But at the moment I have a lot of reading to do, and you should be getting out of here before Dale comes back and finds us together."

"Maybe I should stay," she said vindictively. "He might fire you for betraying his confidence."

"In that case both he and you would lose the best investigator either of you is ever likely to meet, and the mysteries of the past will remain shrouded in mist."

"Pretty sure of yourself, aren't you?"

Matt shrugged carelessly. "Just stating the facts. And if you hang around here much longer, taunting me with your fragrance and beauty, you're going to find out just how sure of myself I am—and why."

Kate blinked and edged toward the open door, feeling the heat of his blatantly sensual gaze. But she wasn't about to leave without letting him know how unfair he was being. She not only had a right to know something was being done, she had a right to be in on it from start to finish.

"That's it, then?" she asked. "Just pat me on the head, say you're checking into it, and tell me to get lost?"

"There are other parts of you I'd rather pat," he said, then sighed loudly as she just stared at him stonily and waited for an answer. "You wanted to know Fidelity was doing something and they are. What else could you ask for?"

She faced him squarely, trying to ignore how powerfully disarming he was. "I could ask—or even demand—that you keep in close contact with me."

"Oh, Kate," he said, his voice low and husky, "staying in close contact with you sounds like exactly what I have in mind."

"Is that the price you charge for keeping me informed of what's going on?" she shot back.

Matt stiffened visibly and his smile disappeared. "Now you listen to me—"

"No," she interrupted, anger coloring her cheeks, "you listen to me. Dale will never admit it, but you and he both know this discreet inquiry, as you're calling it, would never have come about if it hadn't been for suspicions I voiced in the past. Now that it's begun, I assure you I'll continue to be a pain, because Fidelity's sudden willingness to check into my husband's death confirms what I've known all along." Her voice was vehement. "Paul died because of something he knew or was about to find out. He didn't die by accident. Someone killed him, and I won't rest until justice has been done."

Frowning, Matt searched her face, troubled by her outburst. "Justice, Kate?" he asked quietly. "Is that what you want? It sounds to me like you're after revenge."

"I'm after the truth."

"So am I." He lifted his hand to touch her cheek, thought better of it, and let it drop to his side. "I'm not as prone to jumping to conclusions as you seem to be, but if there's something nefarious going on, I assure you I'll find out about it."

Kate looked at him, at his imposing size and hard, unyielding expression. She nodded slowly. "I believe you will, Matt." She felt drawn to this powerful, capable man, and couldn't deny the resounding chord his self-confidence and reassurance struck deep within her.

Something in her eyes must have mirrored her thoughts, because this time when he reached out to touch her he didn't stop himself. He caressed the gentle arch of her neck with his fingertips, enjoying the way she shivered beneath his touch.

"I'll tell you what I believe, Kate," he said in a voice full of sensual promise. "I believe that if we try hard enough, we might even be able to find something else along the way."

"Such as?"

"I think you know perfectly well what I'm talking about. I also think there will come a time when you'll want it to happen just as much as I do right now."

She pushed his hand away. "That, Mr. Gage, is a task even a man like you will find hard to accomplish."

Before she could ask herself what had possibly made her challenge him like that, Kate turned on her heel and strode down the hall, leaving him standing there with a very perplexed expression on his hard, handsome face.

CHAPTER THREE

It hadn't been a good night. Kate had tossed and turned, plagued by dreams she thought she'd seen the last of a year before. When sunrise came she was up to greet it, a mug full of strong tea in her hand and a vague feeling of helplessness surrounding her heart. Something was finally being done, and all she could do was wait.

She hadn't been lying last night when she told Matt she wasn't grieving any longer. Paul had been a good man, a kind man, full of integrity and loyalty to her and the people he worked with. She had felt his loss strongly, but she was a survivor, and a firm believer that life was for the living.

They had been very much in love when they were married. Leaving the insurance company hadn't bothered her at all. In many ways her job there had just been a means to an end, something to do to pay the rent until she found the right man or something better came along. Paul had been the right man—or so she had thought.

People changed. Kate certainly had. It took a year or so, but the role of homemaker just didn't seem to suit her. Perhaps if they had been successful in their attempts to start a family things would have been different. But they remained childless, Paul remained dedicated to his job, and Kate found herself searching for new directions.

Her growth didn't sit well with Paul. He didn't share her concern over their apparent inability to have babies. According to him, he was too busy building his career at the moment to spend enough time with a child anyway. Nor did he share her sudden interest in foreign languages or the return to school that same interest prompted. And he certainly didn't share her enthusiasm over becoming a free-lance translator and the independence that occupation might grant her.

Paul wanted her home, where she belonged.

She studied, he worked, both becoming preoccupied with their own endeavors to help them ignore the way they were gradually drifting apart. And they fought, neither giving an inch, a destructive process that slowly took its toll. A divorce, though never discussed, loomed in the future.

They were to finally sit down to hash it all out when Paul returned from Tucson and the adjustment of a life insurance claim he had described several times as being suspicious and a bit bizarre. They didn't get the chance.

"If only . . ." Kate mumbled to herself as she stared out the window at the new day.

The sound of the doorbell startled her and she spilled her tea, the tepid liquid splashing everywhere. She dried her bare feet, then went to see who was at the door, cursing the damp spots on her jeans and the front of her pale blue sweatshirt.

"Cleaning house at this hour?" Matt asked when she opened the door and he saw her disarray.

"What are you doing here?"

He sighed heavily. "You sound like a broken record, Kate. What am I doing here? What was I doing in Dale's office?" Matt mimicked her wary tone. "I'm working, that's what I'm doing."

Kate still stood on the threshold, her hand on the edge of the door. "At this hour of the morning?"

"You, Kathryn Asher, are a very suspicious woman."

"I simply meant that I find it unusual for you to come calling so early in the day. Did you stop to think I might still be in bed?"

Matt grinned slyly. "I confess the thought did occur to me. The idea of you coming to the door scantily clad and sleepy-eyed appealed to me." He looked forlorn as his eyes roamed over her attire. "But since you're dressed and apparently ready to meet the world, I guess I'll have to settle for making this visit strictly business."

"I see." She stared at him, not knowing what to make of this outrageous man and his seemingly endless seductive banter. "You'd have had to settle for strictly business in any case, I'm afraid. And for your information, I look terrible when I first wake up."

He hummed doubtfully. "I'll be the judge of that. Eventually."

Kate closed her eyes and shook her head. "Does anything throw you off your stride, Matt?"

"Very little. May I come in?"

From the determined expression on his face, Kate knew he would come in whether she wanted him to or not. She shrugged and opened the door wider, stepping back to let him pass. He looked around her living room, his alert eyes taking in the cozy decor and modern furnishings. He nodded appreciatively.

"Very nice."

"Thank you."

It felt odd to have him in her home. She knew she should feel more self-assured on her own turf, but somehow it didn't work out that way. He seemed like an invader, a handsome one that continually stated his intention to seduce her at some unspecified future date. Why *her?* she wondered silently.

"Unusual assortment of reading material," Matt remarked thoughtfully as he scanned the built-in walnut bookshelves lining one wall of the spacious living room. "Spanish, French, German." He turned and looked at her appraisingly. "I wasn't aware you were a linguist."

Kate smiled, feeling more at ease discussing her passion for languages. "Hardly an expert, but I get by. I've been a student at Arizona State University off and on for the past four years."

"Sounds serious."

"I love it, but yes, I'm serious about my studies. I do some document translating now and then, attend discussion groups whenever I can to sharpen my skills with the spoken languages."

"Escort foreign dignitaries?"

She laughed. "That's a very competitive field. The people who do that have usually spent half their lives in the countries where the target language is spoken. If the opportunity to do some real interpreting presented itself, though, I'd grab it like that." She snapped her fingers.

"Paul must have been very proud of you," Matt said, frowning curiously when her smile disappeared.

"Not really."

Kate turned abruptly and led the way to the kitchen. "Watch that spot on the floor," she warned. "I spilled my tea when you rang the bell. I'm not accustomed to such early visitors."

"I'm sorry." He stepped over to where she stood looking at the floor and put his hand lightly on her shoulder.

"It's just a spill." She could feel the warmth of his touch through the material of her top. It made her stomach do a quick, disconcerting flip. "I'll get a rag—"

"I didn't mean the tea, Kate," he interrupted, staying her movements and turning her to look into her eyes. "I meant I was sorry for bringing up a painful subject. Your husband didn't like your outside interests much, did he?"

"If you're sorry for bringing it up, why pursue

it?" Pulling away from him, she went to the sink to get a rag.

Matt watched her clean up the spilled tea, enjoying the way her jeans molded to her body but trying to keep his mind on track. "Because I'm interested in you, Kate. I want to know more about you."

More? He wanted to know everything about her. He hadn't stopped to ask himself why. All Matt knew was that Kate intrigued him, practically beguiled him, and he was enjoying the slow but steady progression of their verbal sparring matches more than he could fathom.

The sight of her bent over like that as she cleaned the floor was more than any man could stand. Of their own accord his hands reached out to caress the fullness of her gently swaying hips.

"What the—" Kate jumped up and whirled around to face him, the skin beneath her jeans feeling scorched by his touch.

"I couldn't help myself." He looked at her, his hands held out in an admission of guilt. "It's all your fault though. I was teased beyond my control."

Her fault? And men spoke of the ambiguity of women's logic! "Well, you'd better learn to control your urges or—"

Matt pulled her into his arms, heedless of her struggles to escape him. She felt trapped as his hands returned to her hips, shaping, caressing, pulling her against his hardness.

"Or you'll what?" he taunted, his lips moving closer to hers by the moment.

"I'll . . ." Kate trailed off, feeling her senses come alive beneath his sensual onslaught, finding herself wanting the kiss he was determined to give her.

Their lips met, and she felt herself melt against him as his tongue darted into her mouth, tasting and probing. When his hands wandered beneath the back of her shirt, however, she seemed to regain some small amount of control and pushed away from him.

"Mmm," he murmured. "If that's the dire consequence for not controlling my urges, I do believe I'll lose control more often."

"Do that again and I'll bite your tongue," she promised, trembling from the desire coursing through her. The heat of his hands and lips still lingered where he had touched her.

She could tell by the way he laughed that he didn't take her threat seriously. Why should he? She had kissed him back, and he could probably sense that the urges within her were as far from angelic as his own. Deep inside, a smoldering fire was growing larger, but she wasn't ready to deal with him yet—if she ever would be.

Turning away as she felt the heat of a bright red blush rising in her face, Kate finished mopping up, returned the rag to the sink, then turned to look at him as he took a seat at the kitchen table. It was as if nothing had happened.

Looking cool and casual in a short-sleeved sport shirt and khaki slacks, his tan deep and his powerful muscles evident, he was a big man who gave the impression of being perfectly in control of everything around him. None of his larger-than-life quality had disappeared in the light of day.

He wanted her, that was quite evident. But there seemed to be more to it than simple desire. He was interested in her too; she could see it in his eyes, just as she had seen it the night before when he had listened to her explanation for prowling around the Fidelity building.

If anything, though, that interest and apparent concern for her emotional state over her late husband worried her more than anything else. She was far from certain of her ability to continue fending off his advances, but she was even less sure of her ability to defend herself emotionally against such a forceful personality.

"Would you like some coffee?" she asked, feeling the need to give herself something to do with her hands.

"I prefer tea as well, please," he replied, chuckling. "And I'm not letting you off the hook that easily. I want to know more about Paul and you."

She poured him a mug of tea and refilled her own before joining him at the kitchen table and asking warily, "Is your interest personal or professional?"

Good question. Matt answered it as best he could. "A little of both, Kate." He looked into her eyes, piercing blue and intelligent, feeling something stir within him. "For the moment at least. I need to check all the angles, get to know this thing from the inside out. I also want to get to know you." He took a sip of his tea and smiled. "Just as thoroughly."

There it was again, that teasing yet blatantly erotic threat. By the way her traitorous body had reacted to his touch a moment ago, she knew just how real that threat was. Fighting him off was becoming increasingly like struggling in quicksand; the more she struggled the deeper she sank.

In a way, however, Kate would rather deal with his sensual banter than his probing questions. Oddly enough it felt safer somehow, less threatening. She shrugged.

"As a friend of Paul's from way back, Dale was obviously aware our marriage wasn't on the best of footings. He told you we'd hit a rocky spot. The rocks were mainly my interest in becoming more than Paul's wife and his certainty that those interests would break us apart," she told him. "Looking at it that way, I suppose he was right."

"Surely you don't blame yourself for that?" Matt asked. "Your need to grow as a person should have strengthened your marriage, not destroyed it. Everybody has to grow, Kate."

She looked at him, still surprised that such a large, tough-looking individual could also be so understanding. "I think he knew that, deep down. He was just afraid of losing me, I guess. I felt the same way, really. We were both growing, but we were growing apart, and instead of taking that fact and dealing with it, we ignored it until it was too late to make the necessary changes—if indeed there were any we could have made."

"Had you discussed divorce?" he asked.

Kate shook her head. "We were probably going to when he got back." Her voice trailed off and she looked at him, suddenly aware of having told him more than she had intended. "How does this help your investigation?"

"Inquiry, please," he reminded her with a humorous frown. "And I've found that even the most unrelated details can sometimes be the most important ones. Besides"—he reached across the table to stroke the back of her hand—"talking about it seems to be helping you, and ultimately that's what this is all about, isn't it?"

"Is it?"

"Of course," he replied innocently.

Kate looked at him doubtfully. He had a way of turning a conversation in any direction he wished, could twist things around to suit his needs. Matthew Gage, she decided, was indeed a very dangerous man. She wondered what his goal was now, and if she'd see it coming in time to put her guard up.

"Just what is your occupation, Matt?"

"I have done—and been called—all sorts of things, usually in a troubleshooting capacity. I suppose right now you could say I'm more of a private investigator than anything else. Naturally, though, with the insurance industry's usual penchant for obscurity, I have been given the official title of independent field claims adjuster," he explained, laughing. "I've got credentials not unlike your late husband's. I just never got the hang of working under the kind of supervision he had to deal with, I guess."

"Hmm."

Matt grinned. "As I said earlier, Kate, you have a very suspicious nature."

"And you, Matt, have a very *mysterious* nature."

"Me?" He gazed at her innocently. "I'm an open book."

"Written in a language I can't read." Yet. "But I'm very good with languages. I'll figure you out, Matthew Gage. You just wait and see."

She had meant the remark as a thinly veiled threat, a warning that she intended to remain on top of the matter and continue to ask questions no matter how he felt about her involvement. To her great surprise he tilted back his head and laughed.

"And you call me mysterious?" he managed, still chuckling. Then he looked at her, his expression more serious. "I'm looking forward to your research, Kate. I really am. Just keep in mind that mysteries are something I'm extremely good at solving. I'll figure you out, too."

That was what she was worried about. He was awfully good at getting close to her, that was for sure. They sat for a moment sizing each other up.

"What did you mean when you said that helping me was the ultimate goal of this . . . inquiry?"

"It does sound overly altruistic, doesn't it?"

She nodded. "Especially coming from you. I'm

sorry, but I get the feeling that you're not a very nice man, Matt," she said, although she wasn't the slightest bit sorry for telling him how she felt.

"I'm really a pussycat when you get to know me."

"Sure you are," Kate said derisively. "A pussycat who could quite probably lift my refrigerator with one hand."

Matt sighed. "Typecast by my size again."

"Hardly. That's the scary part. If you were all brawn and no brains you'd be easy to deal with. But you're not. You're intelligent, articulate, and tricky as the devil. Like a steamroller with a mind of its own and an IQ of one ninety."

"All right. So I can take care of myself verbally and physically. In the kind of situations I seem to get myself into from time to time, those are both qualities I'm glad I have. But I'm not hard to deal with, Kate." He looked into her eyes as he spoke. "And I really am a nice guy."

"As long as people stay out of your way, right?"

"That's essentially correct."

"At least you're honest about that if nothing else."

Matt sighed again and rubbed his chin with his hand. If he was going to get anywhere, either with the job at hand or the more pressing matter of his planned seduction of this intriguing woman, he would have to gain her trust.

"I've been honest with you, Kate. I told you last night that I don't take kindly to interference.

From anyone. I've been hired to do a job and I'll do it—my way." He looked at her pointedly. "But I'm not trying to trick you when I say that Gloria Tynly and you are the important factors here," he added, trying to regain control of the conversation.

Kate let him change the subject again. Since he was bent on pursuing her, she had the feeling there would be plenty of opportunities to figure him out.

"Go on," she prompted.

"You get peace of mind, finally knowing one way or the other about your husbands' deaths. Fidelity will benefit of course: insurance companies are notoriously preoccupied with the truth, especially where claims are concerned."

Kate gazed at him intently. "It sounds to me like you've started to form your own suspicions about what's going on. Did you come across anything interesting in that mountain of files I left you with last night?"

"Let's just say I'm starting to see some rather unusual patterns in the claims your husbands were looking into before their accidents."

"Such as?"

"I came here to get answers, Kate," he told her in a blunt, warning tone. "Not to give them."

"Well, pardon me." She affected a wounded air. "I thought you said this inquiry was mainly for my benefit. I guess I'm supposed to be thankful for small favors and keep my mouth shut, right?"

Matt chuckled and shook his head. "You're good. You really are. Given half a chance I'll bet you might have gotten somewhere with this mess at that."

"Does that mean you're going to take me into your confidence?" she asked innocently.

"It means," he replied sternly, "that I'm going to have to be even more careful about what I say around you."

Kate rose from the table with a disgusted sigh. "Come on, Matt. We're on the same side, after all. What harm can it do to keep me informed?"

He watched in amusement as she poured them both more tea, her movements tense and irritable. "You have a tendency to take a little information and make rash conclusions, that's what harm it can do," he told her, heedless of the way she glared at him when she returned to her seat. "Give you a couple of facts and a few coincidences and you turn it into a conspiracy with cold-blooded killers lurking behind every saguaro cactus in the Sonoran desert."

"But you said you suspected—"

He held a hand up to cut her off. "See? Rash conclusions. I said I was beginning to see some unusual patterns in some life insurance claims. That's a far cry from conspiracy, Katie dear, and a very long way from turning accidents into murder."

"As closemouthed as you are, admitting to that much is proof enough you don't believe in coincidences any more than I do," she said curtly. "And don't call me Katie."

"I suppose it doesn't really fit you." His eyes raked over the swell of her breasts beneath her shirt. "You've got too much fire bottled up inside you."

Choosing to ignore both his desirous gaze and his sensual taunt, Kate sat back in her chair, her arms crossed over her chest, her lips drawn into a thin, tight line.

"I hate this, too," she bit out through clenched teeth. "I hate being on the outside. Has it occurred to you I might actually be able to help you?"

"Why do you think I'm here?"

"I'm beginning to wonder about that," she replied, giving him a sidelong glance. "For a meeting you said was going to be strictly business, this one doesn't seem to be getting much accomplished."

Matt smiled. "On the contrary, Kate, I think we've accomplished quite a bit. For instance, I've discovered you're decidedly grumpy in the morning, probably because you haven't eaten. Why don't we have breakfast together?"

"Fat chance! I wouldn't cook for you if you were the last man on earth."

"Then let's go out," he said, unperturbed by her open hostility. "Some place expensive," he added as he stood up and pulled her to her feet. "On Fidelity's account, naturally."

Kate was hungry, and couldn't deny that the thought of sticking Dale Johnson with a whopping breakfast tab appealed to her no end. She smiled in spite of herself.

"You're on an expense account?"

He nodded slyly. "A big one."

"I'll go change."

CHAPTER FOUR

Kate sighed happily. "I'm stuffed!"

"The best is yet to come," Matt said, motioning for the waiter. He pulled out a company credit card and put it on the spotless white tablecloth alongside the check. "Dale's going to come unglued when he sees this bill."

They laughed together, enjoying the last of a steaming pot of Earl Grey tea and the intimate atmosphere of the elegant Scottsdale restaurant. It had been a sumptuous meal, decadent really, considering the early hour, with fresh baked French pastries and other European breakfast delicacies. Kate had to translate the menu for Matt, a service which had intimidated her late husband but Matt seemed to enjoy immensely.

"Say something in French," he asked her. She did, and he grinned roguishly. "That sounded sexy. What did you say?"

"I called you a horse's rear end," she replied, laughing throatily.

"Is that what I get for buying you breakfast?"

"No, that's what you get when you insist on keeping secrets from me."

Matt wondered if he'd ever get used to how blue her eyes were. Crystal clear, they seemed to mirror her emotions. Of all the moods he'd seen her in thus far, he liked this one best; in spite of her derisive comments about his secrecy, she was happy, teasing, perhaps just a little flirtatious.

"I'm surprised they let me in without a tie."

She looked him over. "You look nice enough. For breakfast at least. From the look of this place I doubt they'd even let you in the parking lot without a tux at dinner time."

"You look nice too." Nice was hardly the word. Lightly tanned and lovely, she was wearing a turquoise-and-gold-colored short-sleeved cotton knit sweater and matching skirt, stylish and cool, perfectly accentuating her slim, athletic, yet very feminine figure.

"Are you going to keep it up?" she asked.

He reluctantly interrupted his rapt contemplation of the gentle swell of her breasts and looked at her face. "I've never had any problems in that department."

"Will you be serious? I meant your secretive behavior."

"Oh. When I know something for certain I suppose I'll let you in on it," he replied. "It's the way I work, Kate. I'm a very methodical person."

He was certainly methodical in his perusal of her physical attributes. "I can see that you are," she remarked dryly. "But wouldn't it help to kick things around some?"

Matt shrugged. With most people a shrug was

a barely noticeable comment of indecision. With the size of his shoulders, however, for him the gesture was more of a major statement, like somebody waving a flag to get attention. This time it seemed to mean he'd come to a decision.

"Okay. But you'll probably find it pretty one-sided."

She sighed with relief. "Anything."

"Did Paul tell you much about the case he was working on before the accident?"

Kate frowned. "It was a life insurance claim—he handled those almost exclusively—a rather large one," she replied thoughtfully. "But that's about as much as I was privy to. He did say it was bizarre, different, something like that."

"That it was," Matt said, nodding his head slowly. "A private plane crash, only the insured aboard, his body . . ." He trailed off and looked at her apologetically. "Suffice it to say the aircraft was not only fully fueled, it was also loaded with explosives."

"What?"

"The insured was a prospector of sorts, a mining entrepreneur on his way to a remote site. The plane blew up and burned so fiercely that all that was left of the poor guy were his dentures."

"I'm surprised Fidelity was willing to insure someone with such a dangerous occupation," Kate said.

"Almost anybody can get insurance if they're willing to pay the premiums."

Kate nodded. "I suppose. If I remember correctly, the company eventually paid the claim, didn't they?"

"Yes. To the tune of a million dollars."

Kate whistled softly. "I'll bet that stuck in Dale's craw. That's probably a part of the reason he refused to talk about it."

"Probably," Matt agreed with a crooked smile. "But Fidelity is a well-based company. They can take that kind of loss and then some."

"True. I doubt they were cheerful about it, though. No wonder Paul spent so much time digging on that case." She nodded thoughtfully.

"I'd give anything to see his preliminary reports. But his accident was fiery too, and whatever findings he may have recorded were lost." Matt was looking at her expectantly, waiting to see if she jumped to conclusions again.

Kate almost spoke her mind, but stopped herself when she saw his expression. "Coincidences do happen," she said in a flat tone.

"You're learning." He grinned at her.

"It was also a coincidence that David was the one who took over that claim."

Matt nodded, knowing what she was leading up to and letting her, wanting to find out if she had really given this situation as much thought as she said she had.

"Not really that much of a coincidence when you think about it, though," she continued. "He was Paul's protégé in a way. He had done some field training with Paul; they worked out at the same club and discussed cases together. He was a natural choice to take over that claim."

The information surprised Matt, but he kept a straight face. "Oh, really?"

Kate wasn't buying his innocent routine. "See? I can give you the kind of stuff you'll never find in the files."

"I would have gotten it eventually," he told her, making a show of stifling a yawn. "From Dale or somebody at the company. Or Gloria Tynly." He glanced at his watch. "I'll be talking to her later."

Her eyes narrowed. "Not without me you won't."

"Now wait just a minute. I'm willing to hash this out with you a little bit, but don't start assuming you're a part of some nonexistent team."

"I'm not. Gloria's a friend of mine and still very distraught. She'll call me the instant you make an appointment with her anyway, so I'll be there with her in any case," she said sharply. "I don't need your permission to lend support to a friend, Matt."

He held up his hands in surrender. "All right. I'm not going to interrogate her, you know. I just want to talk to her."

"And I'll be there when you do."

"Fine."

"Fine." Kate glared at him for a moment, but he kept smiling serenely at her and she finally calmed down. "I suppose you consider it a coincidence as well that the case Gloria's husband was working on when he drowned was also a life insurance claim, another big one, and again a case where no body was actually recovered?"

Matt's eyes narrowed perceptibly. "How do you know all that?"

"Unlike Paul, David had already filed his reports. He had copies at home, and I peeked at them before one of Dale's agents came to take them away."

"You're just full of surprises, aren't you?"

"Answer my question. Don't you find it suspicious that when they died they were both working on large claims involving rather bizarre circumstances?"

"I find it . . ." Matt's voice trailed off and he frowned. "Unusual. But need I point out that that's the kind of claim Gloria's husband routinely handled, just like Paul? And highly trained, experienced divers found enough grisly evidence to conclude that the insured's body had been sucked into one of the underwater caves that area of Florida is dotted with," he added, his voice convincing though he was still frowning.

"I'm aware of the experts' findings. I'm also aware that Fidelity concurred—and paid," Kate said. "But David wasn't scuba diving too close to a dangerous cave. He was simply enjoying a dip on a hot day after checking the accident site and questioning witnesses, a powerful swimmer within a hundred feet of shore."

"For heaven's sake, Kate. A person can drown in his or her own bathtub when—"

"When he or she has been rendered unconscious," she finished. "That's my point."

"You're doing it again," Matt cautioned. "Yes, he had received a blow to the head. No, there weren't any *apparent* obstructions near him. But once again it was the consensus of people who deal regularly with such accidents that he had undoubtedly struck his head on either a floating piece of debris or a rock while diving in the shallows."

"Bull!"

Matt sighed. "I know. You think some evil person or persons unknown sneaked up on him, bashed him on the noggin, and left him to drown, right?"

"I'm simply saying the whole thing was fishy, no pun intended," Kate replied, leaning back in her seat to look around the restaurant with a sulking air. "Let's get out of here. I have the feeling I'm going to start yelling at you in the near future and I don't want to make a spectacle of myself."

In Matt's rather fancy four-wheel-drive truck on the way back to her house, Kate finally regained her composure without resorting to venting her frustrations on him. He remained calm and silent, evidently deep in thought.

"I know I'll probably regret this, seeing as how we've managed to go an entire ten minutes without arguing," Matt said at last, "but I have to ask you about Paul's accident. It's not too painful for you to discuss, is it?"

"No. As you know, it's been two years since it

happened, and I've been over it enough with the authorities at the time and in my mind since."

She looked at him, realizing that he had waited to ask until he knew her better, was more sure of her emotional state. His consideration pleased her, as did the knowledge that he was now aware she was fully prepared to deal with him—in whatever capacity he had in mind.

Though she was trying not to, Kate was starting to like him. She'd like him even more if he weren't so pigheaded, but she'd take that a step at a time in the methodical manner he seemed to prefer. As for the increasingly obvious matter of their mutual attraction—well, she supposed they'd take that a step at a time too.

"Thank you for being so considerate, though," she added. "I'm sorry for implying that you'd browbeat Gloria."

Matt took his attention from the traffic long enough to glance at her, startled by her apology and surprised at the tentative smile on her face. Maybe she was coming around after all. He smiled back.

"Part of the job description. We investigators have to be tactful."

"Some are, some aren't," she said, looking at him doubtfully, then continuing before he could take offense. "Paul was." Kate watched as he carefully signaled a lane change and maneuvered around a slower car, looking in the rearview mirror and turning his head to check for blind spots as he did so. "He was a cautious driver, too, like you are. Very levelheaded, always in control."

"Here we go," Matt muttered. "A barren stretch of road on a dark Arizona night, the monotonous drone of the tires on dry pavement. Even the most careful driver can get highway hypnosis, Kate."

"I know. That's what the highway patrol said. He could have drifted off to sleep, or simply been temporarily distracted when an animal wandered into his path and made him jerk the wheel."

Matt nodded. "That's right. Any of a dozen things. The coroner . . ." He paused to make sure he wasn't disturbing her. "Paul hadn't been drinking, so that was out."

"He didn't drink. He didn't smoke. He didn't drive when he was sleepy. Seat belts were a must with him and he insisted everyone with him wear them too." Kate looked at Matt and added in a serious, quiet voice. "And Paul never, ever went over the speed limit."

"But—"

"There was some question as to whether the claim on his policy was valid," Kate interrupted, "because skid marks showed he was going almost eighty, insane for that section of the road. But despite our problems it was ruled he hadn't been depressed, and vehicular suicides rarely hit the brakes to leave skid marks in the first place."

"He may have been in a hurry to get home to you," Matt said, the excuse sounding lame even to his ears.

"That's what the police and even Dale assumed. In view of the fact that we were most likely going to have yet another in our long string of arguments, however, I would imagine he would have been dragging his feet, not rushing."

"Still—"

"I know," Kate said sarcastically. "Unusual and mysteriously coincidental, but still inconclusive."

They drove along in silence for a time, following their own trains of thought. At last Kate looked over at him, about to make another try at convincing him her suspicions were well-founded. She was surprised to see by his expression that he was already deeply troubled.

"You look perturbed, Matt," she remarked, trying not to sound overly triumphant. "Don't tell me I've actually managed to plant some doubt in that methodical brain of yours."

"You've made a good start," he admitted distractedly. "But there is another, more convincing argument being made on your behalf at the moment." His eyes shifted to the rearview mirror and his frown deepened.

Confused, Kate suddenly took note of their surroundings. She had been so deep in thought she hadn't realized where they were going. "Are you lost?" she asked. "This isn't the way to my house."

"I was just confirming something," he replied.

"What?"

"Remember when I said I'd tell you when I found out something conclusive?" he asked. Kate nodded. "Well, I'm not yet prepared to say there's a conspiracy, nor am I willing to admit the connections between these odd claims and accidents are anything but coincidence, but there's one thing I'm absolutely positive about."

"And that is?"

Matt jerked his thumb over his shoulder. "We're being followed."

CHAPTER FIVE

Kate looked over her shoulder at the white Jaguar sedan behind them, then at Matt, feeling a tingling sensation in the tips of her fingers.

"You've got to be kidding. Who would want to follow us?" she asked.

"Now there's a good question," he replied, calmly turning onto a quiet residential street. The houses were all large, ranch-style dwellings with carefully maintained lawns and citrus trees lining the driveways. "We don't know enough about what's going on to even find anybody's toes, let alone step on them."

"That's right. It's probably just a coincidence."

"I thought you didn't believe in coincidences?"

She didn't. But at the moment it was better than thinking about the alternative. She sat like a statue, watching the scenery roll by as Matt turned left, then right, took another right turn at a red light on Indian School Road and increased his speed slightly, heading back the way they had come.

"You're just trying to scare me, convince me to keep my nose out of this," Kate told him. But when she looked back again, the white car was still behind them.

"Sure I am. And the two guys in that Jag just like to drive in circles," he replied.

Kate sighed. "All right. You win. Are you going to try to outrun them?"

"In Scottsdale? I don't think the local gendarmes would find that amusing, do you?"

"How can you be so jolly?" She glared at him. He was smiling. "You're enjoying this!"

"I guess I am at that," he admitted. "I like it when the opposition makes the first move, especially when they do it badly. Saves me a lot of digging."

He whipped the elegant-looking yet obviously capable four-wheel-drive truck around yet another corner and accelerated down the same quiet street they had been on moments earlier. Kate risked another peek behind them. The white car was still there.

"You're making me dizzy."

"Them too, I hope."

"I think I'm going to be sick," she informed him, gripping the edge of the seat, her eyes wide with panic.

"Not on my custom upholstery you're not."

Kate saw him shift in his seat, his eyes intent on the rearview mirror. His smile had become a wide grin. "What are you going to do?"

"Have a word with them. Hold tight!"

"Don't—"

Matt hit the brakes. Kate closed her eyes, bracing herself for the impending collision. Evidently, however, Matt was just as skilled at this kind of thing as he was at everything else. She heard the squeal of tires on hot pavement, felt a slight bump, and that was all.

When she opened her eyes, Matt was already out of the truck and stalking back to confront the astonished driver of the Jaguar. Kate rolled down her window so she could hear what was going on, feeling a rush of hot air enter the cool interior along with Matt's strident voice.

"You idiot! Look at my bumper. You've scratched the chrome," he said for the benefit of any curious onlookers.

The driver seemed dazed. He sat there, looking at the crumpled front end of his car, then turned his head to watch the big man he'd been following bend down and knock on his window. He rolled it down a crack.

"I'd like a word with you two," Matt told them quietly.

"Oh, brother," the man mumbled.

"Cripes!" his companion agreed. "Let's get out of here!"

Miraculously, the engine of the white Jaguar was still running, but the driver turned the ignition key anyway, wincing when he heard the starter drive gear grind on the spinning flywheel. He fumbled with the gearshift without using the clutch and the transmission added its own grinding complaint.

"Are you going to get out and talk, or would you like to torture this fine car some more?" Matt asked derisively.

"We don't have anything to talk about," the driver replied, still trying to jam the car into gear.

"Then I'll just have to come in and get you." Matt put his hands through the small space at the top of the driver's window and pushed, forcing it down inside the door with a crunch. "There now. Isn't that better? It's a lovely summer day out here, don't you think?"

"You're a nut case!" the driver complained. "We were just driving along, minding our own business—"

"And just what is your business?" Matt interrupted.

"What's it to you?" the passenger shot back, feeling safer than the driver because he was out of Matt's reach.

Or so he thought. Matt put his arm into the car and grabbed the man by his carefully knotted silk tie, pulling him as far into the driver's lap as the seat belt he was wearing would allow. Matt's shoulders wouldn't fit through the window, so he settled for leaning as far into the car as he could, bringing his face within inches of the other man's.

"I asked you a question. Why were you following us? Who do you work for?"

His face was turning red. "Carson—" He gasped when the driver hit him in the ribs.

"Shut up, Angelo."

"Carson who?" Matt demanded.

"You're a dead man," the driver said bitterly as he finally managed to put the gearshift into reverse. "You hear me? You're an accident looking for a place to happen, just like the others."

Matt barely managed to pull his head out of the window before the driver stepped on the accelerator, the car's tires squealing as it backed swiftly away from the rear end of the truck. He heard the gears grind again and jumped out of the way as the car leaped forward, coming within inches of him.

But in his hatred and haste the driver misjudged the clearance as he roared around the truck, hitting the rear bumper again and shearing off the Jaguar's right front fender. Glass from the broken headlight sprayed everywhere, the twisted fender bouncing to a stop near Matt's feet. Looking like a refugee from a demolition derby, the beleaguered white car raced to the end of the block, turned the corner, and was gone.

Matt stood there for a moment, blinking in the bright sunlight and trying to calm down. He looked at Kate, who was staring at him through the rear window of the truck like he was an alien from another planet.

"Are you all right?" he asked. She nodded but didn't say a word.

"Some people," an ancient voice said behind him.

He spun around, then relaxed when he saw a wizened gentleman in bright shorts standing in the middle of a nearby yard. He was watering a towering palm tree, careful not to splash mud on the white-painted trunk.

"Excuse me?" Matt asked politely.

"Some people," the man repeated, "will do anything to keep their car insurance premiums from going up."

Matt chuckled. "Yeah. Sorry about the mess."

"City'll be out to clean it up," the elderly man said, unperturbed. "Nothing stays dirty in this part of town for very long. You might want to take the fender, though." He smiled. "Might as well have a trophy, since you'll never see any cash."

"Good idea." He picked the fender up and put it in the bed of his truck, noticing as he did so that this wasn't the first time the Jaguar had been in a wreck. "A very good idea. Thanks," he said. Then a terrible thought occurred to him. "Uh, you didn't by any chance get the license number, did you?" he asked the man.

"Nope."

"Damn!"

Some hotshot investigator he was. Having a good-looking woman like Kate around must be more of a distraction than he thought.

"Couldn't," the old gentleman continued. "The plates were smeared with mud. Makes you wonder if that's what they do for entertainment."

"What?"

"Go around bashing into people."

"You're incredible," Kate said, shaking her head in disbelief.

"Thank you."

"I wasn't being complimentary."

"Oh."

"I still can't believe you did that," she continued, sinking into a chaise longue in the shade of her backyard patio. "I mean really! Car wrecks, strong-arm tactics. What would you have done if those two had gotten out of the car? Beaten them senseless in the middle of the street?"

"I would have done whatever they forced me to do," Matt replied in a matter-of-fact tone. "All I wanted to do was get their attention and have a chat."

"And what if they had pulled guns on you?"

"These people deal in accidents, not shootings."

"Well, somebody could have gotten hurt."

"Aren't you forgetting who we're dealing with, Kate?" he asked, small lines of irritation forming at the corners of his mouth.

She glared at him. "No. I heard that one man threaten you, tell you you were dead and an accident looking for a place to happen just like the others." She shivered despite the heat. "I realize they're bad men. But we're supposed to be the good guys, Matt. Why do you have to sink to their level?"

"Don't be so naive," he said curtly. "It's been my experience that good only triumphs over evil if good is very, very careful and gets in the first punch."

"What kind of homicidal maniac are you?"

Matt turned abruptly from his thoughtful contemplation of Kate's carefully landscaped backyard and hauled her out of the chaise to her feet. Holding her by the arms and glaring at her, he unleashed on her a small measure of the frustration recent events had brought to a boil within him.

"I'm only going to tell you this one more time, Kate," he began in a chilling voice, "so get it straight. I'm running this show. Period. You are an adviser at best, one whose nuisance value is coming dangerously close to exceeding her worth. I don't want to hear another peep out of you concerning my methods. You're smart and you're crafty but you're an amateur. What you know about dealing with the kind of people who have evidently set their sights on me would fit on the head of a pin."

It was useless to struggle against Matt's iron grip and Kate didn't try. She looked into his eyes, listened to the quiet threat in his voice, and tried not to show how helpless he made her feel.

What really bothered Kate was that he was right; she had no idea how to deal with the kind of people who might be responsible for her husband's death. Matt did, and the thought frightened her. She didn't know whether she should run as far from him as possible or stay as close to his comforting protection as she could.

"All right," she admitted. "So you know what you're doing. I can't deny that. But how can you justify—"

"I had all the justification I needed," he interrupted. "I don't know how they got wind of Fidelity's renewed interest in this mess, but they did. They were just checking me out today, seeing what I was doing and how much of a threat I might be." Matt brought his face even closer to hers. "But they got careless and let me know they were there. They tipped their hand and they know it, making me a mistake they're going to have to try to erase. And you're telling me not to get too rough?"

Somehow, Kate found the strength to glare back at him, though she knew she was trembling as much out of fear as anger at being treated like a fool.

"I wouldn't be so stupid as to try to tell a man like you what to do," she informed him, cursing the way her voice wavered. "It's quite clear to me you're an expert. A real pro at intimidation and violence. If being appalled at what you are makes me an amateur, then I'm glad I am one."

"What a hypocrite you are, Kate," he said, pulling her against him and wrapping his arms around her. "I don't think you're as appalled at the kind of man I am as you'd like to think you are."

Kate struggled, merely succeeding in making herself even more aware of his power, of the way her soft breasts flattened against the broad, muscular expanse of his chest.

"I am!" she objected adamantly.

"I can hear your heart beating, feel your skin warm to my touch," Matt said softly as he stroked her spine with one strong hand. "Face it, Kate. You're not appalled. You're excited."

His embrace had her nearly breathless. "I'm scared of you, that's all," she managed to say, her voice barely more than a whisper.

"You have nothing to fear from me, Kate." He held her even tighter, enjoying the way her body fitted to his. "I won't hurt you. But I think you kind of like being a bit frightened, don't you?"

"No!"

"I'm strong, Kate. Can you feel it? I could take you right now." Easily holding her with one arm around her waist, he lifted her clear of the ground and carried her into the cool interior of her house. Once inside he let her down gently, his hand slipping beneath her top to tease the undersides of her breasts. "I could undress you and take you, Kate. I want to. I've wanted to since the first time I saw you."

Gasping, Kate turned away from his smoldering gaze, feeling her face grow warm with color as his hands sought the full contours of her breasts, molding first one and then the other with maddening deliberation. He hooked his fingers beneath the edge of her colorful knit top and pulled it up over her breasts, then pressed his hard, masculine torso against her bare stomach.

"Stop," she whispered, though a fire had started to burn within her that told her she wasn't at all sure if she wanted him to stop or not. "Please, Matt . . ."

"I could take you," he repeated softly. Matt lifted her chin with his finger and kissed her, his tongue probing her mouth, making its sweet secret places his own. "But I won't. Because I want you to know you don't have to be afraid of me. The next time you say please I want it to be because you want me, not because you want me to stop."

"Damn you," Kate said hoarsely, managing to look at him defiantly though her body betrayed her growing desire. "Do you think you can do whatever you want with me?"

"You know I can," he replied, his eyes full of a sensuous, almost evil light. "What's more, deep down, you want me to, don't you?"

He started unbuttoning his shirt. Kate's eyes widened and she shook her head, yet she seemed unable to speak or even turn away from the tan skin he revealed. Matt took her hands and placed them on his bare chest.

"Go ahead, Kate. Touch me. I know you want to."

"I don't!"

But her own hands belied her words. He didn't have to hold them. Her fingertips splayed across his warm skin, gliding across his chest, to his sides, down the flat, hard surface of his stomach. Drawn by some insane, uncontrollable urge, Kate dipped her head to touch her lips against his taut flesh, her tongue darting out to taste him.

Then she came to her senses and jumped back as if burned. "I . . ."

"Go ahead, Kate. Deny it now," he taunted. "I dare you."

"You're despicable!" she cried, dashing past him and out onto the patio, rearranging her clothes as she ran. She hugged herself tightly, trembling, tears of outrage shimmering in her eyes.

Matt joined her. "I never said I wasn't," he agreed. "There's no shame in desire, Kate. We all have needs. How long has it been for you?"

"Just go away," she told him miserably.

"There was more to it than a lack of communication, wasn't there?" he continued. "Paul and you didn't get along too well in other ways, did you?"

"Shut up!"

Kate left the porch and ran out into the yard, sinking to her knees on the soft lawn beside a bed of prickly pear cactus. They were flowering, the yellow blooms appearing very delicate amid the thorny spines. She didn't look at him when Matt came to kneel beside her.

"I'm sorry."

"Are you?" she asked curtly, impatiently brushing tears from her eyes.

Matt smiled and reached out to stroke her hair. "No, I guess not."

"I didn't think so. You'll run roughshod over anyone to get what you want, won't you? And since you want me, you think nothing of stepping all over my feelings in the process."

"You're right about one thing," he replied lazily. "I do want you. And I won't stop until you admit you want me. But you are a tricky problem, Kate." He touched one of the cactus flowers. "Like this bloom. So sweet, so promising, yet nestled among thorns."

She turned her head to look at him, searching his face. Her own expression was openly hostile. "Be careful, Matt. You might get stabbed."

"You see? You're not as peaceful as you pretend to be. It's all a matter of degree, you know. You were willing to break into Fidelity's files to try and find the truth, quite prepared to become a thief in your pursuit of justice."

"I was driven to it," Kate objected.

"Ah. Yet when I resorted to violence because I was confronted by two men who were quite possibly cold-blooded killers, I wasn't being driven to it, right?" he asked dryly.

Kate frowned, trapped by his logic. "It's not the same thing."

"Have it your way," he returned with a sigh. "There are just two things you have to remember, Kate. One is that I will do whatever I have to do to get to the bottom of this mess, whether you approve of how I go about it or not."

Kate watched him stand up, thankful yet vaguely frustrated that the moment of sensual threat seemed to have passed. "And the second?" she asked.

"Since this is getting more dangerous by the moment and your part in it will soon be at an end, the second thing I want you to remember is the one that concerns you the most," he informed her, taking her hand and pulling her up next to him. "I'm also going to do whatever I have to do to unlock all the passion I know you're capable of, Kate. And there won't be a thing you can do to stop me."

The tall, thin man adjusted the cuffs of his pale pink silk shirt until precisely three quarters of an inch protruded past the sleeves of his white tropical suit coat. Standing comfortably in his pristine ivory Gucci loafers, he looked through the broad expanse of glass before him at the calm waters of the Caribbean, some five hundred feet below the bleak, craggy cliffs surrounding his immense villa.

His name was Carson, and Carson was not pleased. When Carson was not pleased, everyone around him put on their long faces. Only one such sorrowful countenance could be seen reflected in the window beside him, because only his most trusted minion had been able to work up the courage to bring him the news.

"So," Carson said quietly.

His minion cringed. "It is a great pity."

Carson nodded slowly, then stood very still for a long time, staring out the window, bringing his devious mind to bear on the problem at hand. The other man stood very still as well, because to interrupt Carson at a time like this would be nothing short of suicide. Carson was a psychopath, a very intelligent, incredibly wealthy psychopath.

Suddenly, Carson smiled. He almost never smiled. It frightened his minion so badly he took a step backward and closed his eyes, saying his prayers and awaiting his fate.

"Open your eyes, you fool," Carson said, his lip curling in disgust. "And listen. I knew the two idiots in Phoenix would fail me eventually. It was inevitable." He shrugged his thin shoulders, looking not through the window but at his reflection, admiring the way his suit hugged his back as he did so. "This man, this Matthew Gage."

"Yes?" his minion asked anxiously, hearing the sudden power and decision in Carson's voice and knowing a chance would be coming to make himself useful.

"Is he smart?"

"Our sources say yes."

"Is he . . ." The man paused, searching for the right word. "Is he dangerous?" He rolled the word off his tongue as if it had a flavor he particularly liked.

His minion was getting excited. He couldn't decide whether to continue looking sorrowful or risk a smile. Settling on something in between he answered, "Again they say yes."

"Good!" It wasn't so much an exclamation as a minor explosion of sound. "The other two were stupid, weak, and unimaginative. To deal with Gage will take talent. He will be good for us, strengthen us." Carson spun around and pointed a bony finger at his minion. "And only the strong survive in this world. Is that not so?"

"It is so," the other man agreed, his heart pounding in his chest. He took another step backward and nearly fell over a chrome-and-glass end table.

Carson nodded, gratified by the other's abject fear and obedience. "This smart man knows something is going on. He doesn't know what, but he will try to find out. This dangerous man will come poking and prodding into my affairs."

"We will arrange an accident?"

"Naturally. But Gage will not be easy to kill. I can feel it. We have grown fat and lazy without any true predators to challenge us. He will die of course, but not before he has tested us, thinned our ranks, and made us leaner, tougher." Carson adjusted his cuffs again and turned placidly back to the window. He smiled, his face like a death's head. "Perhaps he might even make it to me. Then Matthew Gage will have a very bad accident. You see? I am brilliant. I take a failure and turn it into a success."

"Brilliant," his minion agreed, backing toward the door. "Oh. Forgive me. The two in Phoenix said there was a woman with Matthew Gage."

"A woman?"

"They think it is the noisy one from before."

"Yes." Carson's smile grew even more hideous. "Paul Asher's widow. You see? Even she senses the power of this man who has come to test us."

"If she comes with him . . ."

Carson stared out the window. "Now, that," he said, his voice devoid of emotion, "would be a great pity indeed."

CHAPTER SIX

Gloria Tynly lived in Mesa with her rambunctious, healthy baby boy, David Tynly, Jr. Kate introduced them both to Matt and then told Gloria everything that had happened—or almost everything.

Even if Matt hadn't been there listening, how could she begin to explain the growing attraction she felt for the enigmatic investigator? She couldn't tell anyone about the way her heart raced when he touched her, because she didn't quite believe it herself. Nor had she come to grips with the insane desire building within her, the desire to allow herself to be swept along by the passion and sensuality Matt confronted her with at every opportunity.

His questioning of the grieving widow was tactful, his manner surprisingly gentle for a man Kate knew to be capable of frighteningly rough behavior. Satisfied that he was keeping his promise to be nice to Gloria, Kate took little David to play in the living room, giving herself a break from Matt's disturbing presence and Gloria a much-needed respite from the baby's incessant, fussy curiosity.

He was barely six months old, too young to miss his father, really. That would come later, when he was old enough to understand and feel his father's absence. It wasn't fair at all, and Kate felt hatred rise within her toward the people responsible for the senseless loss.

Matt was right. She wasn't as peaceful as she pretended to be. Deep inside her, black emotions twisted and turned. More than the need to see justice done she had a dark dream of revenge. It wasn't pleasant to think about, but she knew it was inside her, waiting.

Ugly and vengeful though it was, it had occurred to her that one reason for sticking close to Matt was his obvious capability for violence. He had vowed to get to the bottom of things, and she knew better than to doubt his ability to do so. When he caught up with these people, he could—and quite possibly would—end up exacting the toll she sought. They wouldn't go happily to jail. Matt would do whatever they forced him to do.

Baby David started to fuss again, so Kate changed him and put him down for a nap. She stayed beside him, kissing away his frustrations until he drifted off, then stood by his crib watching him sleep.

A child might have pulled Paul and her together. If they'd been closer, and if he had wanted to spend more time with the baby, he might not have gone to Tucson that day. At the very least she would have had a son or daughter to comfort her. Gloria had told her that little David was her salvation, her island of hope.

Kate came out of the baby's room to find Matt standing in the living room. He looked restless and very, very angry. "I'm done," he informed her curtly.

"What's wrong?"

"Nothing." Matt ran his hands over his face and sighed. "I'll . . . I'll wait for you in the truck," he said, then quietly left the house.

After making sure Gloria was all right, she kissed the petite blonde on the cheek and said good-bye, then joined Matt outside.

"I thought you would upset her," she said after they had driven some distance in silence. "But she was fine. Knowing you're on the case seemed to put her more at ease, actually."

"She's a strong woman."

"Yes." She looked intently at him. "Did you discover anything by talking to her?"

"Nothing new."

"Is that why you're so mad?"

Matt glanced at her, then away, struggling with his emotions. "Mad?" he repeated, his knuckles white on the steering wheel. "Mad doesn't begin to describe my feelings, Kate. That poor woman, her beautiful baby boy . . . If someone did arrange the accidents that claimed your husband and hers, I swear I don't know what's going to happen to them when I find them."

Not knowing quite what made her do so, Kate reached over and put her hand on Matt's thigh.

He covered it with his own, his large fingers intertwining with hers.

"I thought you said you were going to bring them to justice," she said softly.

"That I will," he promised. "If they're lucky."

Their next stop was a rather majestic-looking auto body shop in Tempe. Matt pulled his truck into a fenced lot behind the polished marble building and got out, waving at an odd little man who walked out to greet him.

"Gage," he said, "what have you done to the truck now?"

"Oh, she got her flanks bruised a bit this morning, but that's not why I'm here, Al," Matt replied amiably. He lifted the crumpled fender out of the pickup bed and showed it to the little man. "I want you to give this the once-over if you've got the time."

"Sure. With resort season over I mostly sit around with my—" He broke off when he noticed Kate sitting in the truck. "Oops. Hello, ma'am."

"Hello."

"Kate, this is Al, the Michelangelo of auto body work," Matt told her. "Al, meet Kate Asher."

"Glad to meet you, ma'am."

"Likewise," she replied, climbing out of the truck. "But if you call me ma'am one more time, you'll be pulling a dent out of your shin."

Al laughed uproariously. "Okay, Kate. Let's step inside the shop out of this sun and I'll take a look at the fender."

Matt hung back to let Kate take the lead,

watching her hips away slightly as she walked across the parking lot. Al slowed his pace and joined him.

"She's built for speed, Matt," the little man whispered appreciatively. "Nice bumpers, too."

"Crass, Alexander. Very crass. But nonetheless true," Matt agreed.

He had calmed down considerably. Holding Kate's hand on the way there had helped. The gesture had pleased him, made him realize that in some ways she was beginning to trust him. It had also, however, made him aware of an almost painful longing for her that could only be relieved in one way—he had to have her, and the sooner the better.

"Put it on the bench over there, Matt," Al instructed, pulling a rolling box of tools closer to the brilliantly lighted work area. He peered at the fender. "Jaguar of course. Older four-passenger sedan, if I'm not mistaken."

"Have you ever been?" Matt remarked.

"Rarely. Let's see, now," Al muttered.

Kate watched, her eyebrows arched, as he bent over the twisted piece of metal with a magnifying glass and a pair of tweezers, humming and clucking his tongue.

She looked up at Matt, who stood gazing intently over Al's shoulder. She concluded that both he and his little friend were as crazy as loons, but watched and listened with rapt attention anyway.

"It's been hit before."

"I noticed," Matt said. "That's why I picked it

up after two gentlemen tried to smear me all over it this morning. I thought it might tell some tales."

"Hmm. My three-year-old granddaughter could have done a better job of priming the metal. See how the layers peel off in strips?" He showed them, holding up a stringy flake of paint with the tweezers. "Cheap enamel too. The work appears to have been done a while ago, though, so I suppose under the circumstances it held up pretty well."

"Any idea who might have done the job?"

"Whoever it was, they were in one heck of a hurry." Al waved his hand. "Lots of poor work out there. I'd say south of the border, though, judging by the way the primer coat smells." He sniffed the paint strip, then held it under each of their noses in turn. "See? Harsh kind of scent, poor quality thinner that leaves odd distillates behind when it evaporates."

"How about the reason for having the work done?"

Al slowly and methodically stripped the peeling paint from the fender, using what looked to Kate like a surgeon's scalpel. If he hadn't appeared so serious about what he was doing, she might have laughed out loud. She glanced at Matt, who smiled at her and winked.

"Here we go," the body man mumbled. "See this?" He motioned them closer to have a look. "They really were in a hurry. Didn't bother to smooth out the scratches. Just pulled a few dents and applied the primer."

"What did they hit?" Kate found herself asking.

"Another car."

She blinked. "I suppose you're going to tell us the make and model of it too, right?"

Al looked up at her and grinned. "What do you think I am? A magician?"

"Well, I . . ."

"I'll have to run a few tests on the paint the other vehicle left behind in these scratches to tell you that."

Matt laughed at the astounded look on her face. "Come on. Let's let Al work and go grab a quick hamburger or something before you embarrass yourself again."

"Who is that guy?" Kate demanded quietly as they strolled out of the air-conditioned shop.

"Just an automobile enthusiast and former government laboratory analyst who retired in Phoenix to operate his own restoration business."

"You have the strangest acquaintances."

"If you want strange, I'll introduce you to a lady in Las Vegas who knows everything there is to know about boa constrictors. She used to use them as part of her nightclub act, and—"

"Please," Kate interrupted. "Spare me the details."

They ran across the street and had a fast-food lunch, then went back to find Al hunched over a microscope. A row of test tubes filled with murky liquids had joined the ordered clutter on the workbench.

When he saw them enter, Al straightened

abruptly, took a seat on the edge of the workbench, and lighted a cigarette. Squinting through the smoke at some nonexistent point in the distance, he was silent for a long time. Kate and Matt waited patiently until he roused himself to speak.

"Mexico, definitely. Probably one of the chop shops just across the border specializing in quick processing of stolen vehicles. The paint scrapings are harder to pin down, but I'd say the Jag hit or was hit by a General Motors product, tan color, recent model," he told them thoughtfully. "Judging by the amount of rust in the dents, the collision took place two, maybe three years ago." He sighed and looked at them. "Sorry, but that's as close as I can come. Do you any good?"

Matt shrugged. "Too early to tell. Food for thought, though," he said. "Thanks, Al. I owe you one."

"You owe me twenty, but who's counting?"

Kate was too astounded by the little man's seemingly magical revelations to say anything, or even to make any connection between what he had said and the matter at hand.

She found her tongue on the way back to her house. "What, pray tell, was that all about?" she asked in a bewildered voice.

"Maybe nothing, maybe a glimmer of a lead," Matt replied thoughtfully.

"Pardon?"

He glanced at her. "Why should I lay it out for you?" he returned brusquely. "You'd probably just make some more wild assumptions, then beat me over the head with them and cloud my thinking."

"Come on, Matt. I think I've behaved quite well when you consider I've been pumped for information, involved in a car wreck, and forced to endure your outrageous attentions while being trotted all over town in this heat," she said bitterly. "Not to mention being ogled and told I have nice bumpers by some mad scientist turned paint and body man."

Matt shook his head and chuckled. "What sharp little ears you have. Al was only being complimentary." He watched the rise and fall of her breasts as she breathed. "And you do have nice bumpers. Front and rear," he added, running his hand along the curve of her hip.

She inched away from him. "Keep your hands—and your bizarre compliments—to yourself. Tell me what's going on."

"Give me one good reason why I should."

"Because . . ." Kate thought furiously, forcing her mind to make some sense out of what she had heard at Al's. Her eyebrows arched and she smiled. *"Usted no tiene español."*

"What?"

"You have no Spanish."

"Spanish what?"

Kate laughed triumphantly. "You don't speak the language. I do. I learned Spanish right along with English in the school I went to, spoke it on the playground with the other kids. If you're planning on going to Mexico to try to find the shop that fixed the Jaguar, you'll need me."

"For your information, dear," he said with a patronizing smile, "the location of the shop is only interesting because it suggests they had to have the work done fast and on the sly. It's hardly a surprise that bad guys in this part of the country would know somebody south of the border who does that kind of thing."

Her shoulder's slumped. "Oh. Then what . . ." What else had he learned at the body shop? Suddenly it dawned on her, and her face turned pale at the thought. "A two-year-old dent, with traces of tan paint in it from a General Motors car." She stared at Matt, feeling sick to her stomach.

"This is what I was afraid of," he muttered. "I can practically hear the little buzzer going off in your head."

"Good Lord! Paul drove a tan Chevrolet. Those two men chased him in that Jaguar, pushed him into a ditch, and killed him!"

"Calm down, Kate," Matt demanded.

"But we know! We have to find them, tell the police, something!" She leaned forward, pointing out the window. "There's a phone!"

"I said calm down!" He reached over and pushed her back in the seat. "In the first place, *we* aren't going to do anything. And in the second, you're making allegations based on evidence so slim the police would laugh you out of the station. That's assuming they wouldn't take one look at the file—a file they consider closed, I hasten to add—remember your name and the suspicions you voiced at the time, and then send you to a shrink."

"But—"

"But nothing," Matt cut her off abruptly. "This information is just what I told Al it was—food for thought. There are a lot of tan GM products around. That Jag may or may not have bumped Paul's car off the road, and if it did those two men may or may not have been involved."

He was furious with her. Kate knew she had to do as he said and calm down. If he got any angrier he might cut off even the tiny amount of consideration he had shown her thus far. She took several deep breaths and nodded. He was, after all, right. She had very little credibility left with the authorities.

"Okay," she said, holding up her hands to show him she accepted his logic. "I'm sorry. But please, please tell me how *you* think this all fits in. Just so I know I'm not crazy."

The muscles on the back of Matt's neck had tightened with anger. He relaxed them. "You're not crazy. You're just not being objective, that's all," he said, his tone of voice returning to normal. "I look at the facts and I see an expensive car that has been poorly repaired because it had to be done quickly and quietly. That points to an accident the owner didn't want anyone to know about. The repair was done in Mexico, suggesting that I need to keep my eye out for any other clues that might lead there."

"And the tan paint?"

"Could have come from anywhere. It was,

however, found in a dent on a car that was following me. The people in that car threatened me. Among other things I am looking into the circumstances surrounding the death of a man who perished in a wreck while driving a tan car."

"It seems to me you've reached the same conclusion I did, only you're putting it in more cautious language," Kate said, trying not to sound too sarcastic.

"I'll say this plainly enough. We're getting in someone's way, Kate. They won't like it. Starting as of now I am proceeding on the assumption that there is some kind of cover-up going on, that it involves Fidelity and millions of dollars, and that whoever is behind it is probably willing to commit murder to keep it quiet."

Kate stared at him. "That's quite an assumption, coming from you."

"It is just an assumption, remember. But to forge blithely ahead without considering all the possibilities would be foolish."

"And where, if I may ask, are you planning on forging ahead to?"

Matt chuckled, pleasantly surprised that she had gotten a grip on herself so quickly. The woman had brains and bravery as well as a sexy body. If by some fluke he did have to keep her with him on this, it was nice to know she might come in handy for more than warm companionship and language skills.

"You may ask. There is one other thing I need from you before I fulfill my promise to continue on without you."

Kate eyed him warily. "Matt," she warned.

"You seem to have forgotten my second promise, Kate," he said, his voice full of quiet sensuality. "When the time comes I won't ask for you, I'll take you, because you'll want me to."

"You pompous, arrogant—"

"In the meantime," Matt continued, "I want you to show me the spot where Paul's car went off the road, just so I can get a feel for the way it might have happened."

Kate folded her arms over her chest. He seemed so sure she would simply fall into his arms. Of course, from the way her entire body tingled at his briefest touch, she wasn't so sure she wouldn't.

"Find it yourself," she muttered.

"I need to know the exact spot, not some vague description from an old police file," he returned. "Then I have to go to Tucson to speak with the widow of that prospector who met his end in the plane crash. It would be a waste of time to haul you back here after you identify the spot, so you'll accompany me to Tucson."

"Be still my heart."

"It will probably be too late to see her when we get there, so we'll make that our first stop tomorrow morning before heading back."

Kate had started to sulk, but her eyes popped open and she glared at him. "You don't mean . . ."

Matt pulled the truck into her driveway and parked. "Need any help packing an overnight bag?" he asked. His eyes held a libidinous gleam as he gazed at her.

"No," she said curtly. "I am not going to Tucson to spend the night with you, Matthew Gage. Forget it."

"Remember to bring along a swimsuit. I know this terrific place with private whirlpools. On second thought, the swimsuit isn't mandatory."

"Didn't you hear me? I'm not going anywhere with you."

"I need you and you're going, even if I have to strap you to the front of the truck, dear."

He would do it, too. She knew him well enough now not to doubt his ability or his resolve. "How can I resist such a kind invitation?"

"Look at it this way: you wanted to be my partner, didn't you?" He grinned as she nodded warily. "Well, this is your last opportunity to be on the front lines."

Though she knew she didn't really have any choice, she did choose to look at it that way. Maybe she could even convince him he needed her help for the duration.

"All right," Kate agreed curtly. She got out of the truck and slammed the door. Hearing his door open, she spun around and held up her hand. "Stay here. I don't want you in my house." She would be doing her packing in the bedroom, and that was the last place she wanted him.

"Get a move on, then." He grinned. "Be out in ten minutes and I'll even get you your own room tonight." He nearly fell out of the truck laughing at the way she turned and dashed into the house. "Of course," he added to himself, "I didn't say anything about staying in my own room, now, did I?"

CHAPTER SEVEN

"Did Paul always take the road through Apache Junction to and from Tucson?" Matt asked.

Kate nodded. "There's more to see," she explained. "The view along the interstate is pretty barren."

"True."

Looking at the scenery around them now, Kate knew that someone accustomed to verdant fields and roaring rivers might consider this route pretty barren too. But she liked the arid landscape, found its power and subtle beauty as pleasant to look at as any of Mother Nature's more fertile creations.

Especially now. The paloverde were in bloom, the eerie green trees covered with tiny yellow flowers a brilliant testimony that the desert was far from lifeless. Many different kinds of cacti were in full bloom as well, dots of color against the background of the desert floor. Added to the various shades of red, green, and orange displayed by many other types of flowering shrubs, bushes, and trees, it was a scene as lovely as a northern spring.

The accident site was a sand-filled wash, harmless-looking save for evidence of the devastating bite rushing water could take out of arid soil during flood times. All traces of the wreck that had taken place there two years before had been obliterated long ago. Preferring not to look at the place again, Kate stayed in the truck while Matt scouted around.

"Not much to see," Matt said as he climbed in beside her and pulled back onto the highway. "But I got what I came for. It's a good place for somebody to push somebody else off the road."

"Are you convinced yet that that's what happened?"

He shrugged. "Just more food for thought."

"You're a hard man, Matthew Gage," Kate remarked.

"Getting harder all the time," he agreed amiably, his thoughtful frown turning into a wolfish grin as he looked over at her. "Want to see?"

"You're incorrigible," she shot back, then held up her hand to cut him off when he opened his mouth again. "Yes, I know. You never said you weren't."

They drove on in surprisingly companionable silence, caught up in their own thoughts, the humming truck eating up the miles. It seemed to take them both by surprise when they noticed they were approaching the sprawling edges of town. New construction blended with the old to create a harmonizing effect. Red tile roofs were abundant along with white, pink, and tan adobe-style buildings.

"Have you been to Tucson before?" Kate asked.

"A few times—enough to know the basic lay-out of the area," he replied, keeping his eyes on the increasing flow of traffic.

Kate looked out at the passing scenery, debating with herself whether or not to bring up the subject. "Where are we staying?"

"Here." He pulled up in front of a new, stylish hotel and nosed the truck into a registration-only parking slot. The vehicle seemed to breathe a sigh of relief when he turned off the engine. "I'll be right back."

She slipped out of the truck along with him. "Separate rooms."

"What?" Matt turned to face her, one eyebrow quirked upward. He wasn't worried. If she wanted her own room, that was fine with him. He would willingly walk farther than a few steps next door for her.

"And I'll pay for my own," she informed him, the bed of the truck still safely between them.

He leaned against the chrome, took off his sunglasses, and eyed her warily. "I'll pay."

"No." Maybe she was being silly, but if he paid she'd feel like a kept woman. "I want to pull my own weight."

Matt shook his head, exasperated with her. "We are not a team, Kate. You wouldn't be here if it wasn't for me. I'll pay all the expenses." His tone conveyed clearly that that was his final word on the subject. But Kate wasn't about to give in that easily.

"No!"

"Would you rather share a room with me?"

She struggled to control her temper. There was no doubt in her mind that he meant what he said. What bothered her most was how unsure of herself she was around him. What did she really want?

"Take your time," he said sarcastically. "It's only about ninety-nine degrees out here."

"You've got at least another minute before you start to melt," she replied angrily, mad at him for looking so clean, crisp, and appealing. Hard as a rock, too—so different from any man she'd known before.

"Kate!"

"All right. Separate rooms, you pay." She fell into step beside him.

"I can do this alone. Or don't you trust me?"

"No, I don't," she retorted as they walked into the cool reception area.

He walked confidently up to the desk. "Two rooms please. I'll take the hot-tub suite, and the lady would like to be close by." He smiled engagingly at the pretty receptionist, then turned to give Kate a sly wink.

She shot him a dirty look, then wandered over to browse through the pamphlets describing things to see in Tucson. It didn't take long before he was back to pester her again.

"Your lonely room awaits you, milady," he whispered in her ear, dangling a key in front of her. "Unless you'd rather slip into mine for a while?"

"Fat chance."

He shrugged. "In that case, let's drop off the luggage and then go find a place to eat."

His voice was low and sexy, almost a caress in itself breezing across her smooth skin. The sudden hardening of her nipples had nothing to do with the combination of hot and cold air hitting her as he held the door open for her.

"I know a good Mexican restaurant nearby," she said, trying to shake off the effects of his closeness.

"Let's go. I'm almost to the point of wasting away before your very eyes."

Kate eyed his bulk with a skeptical look. "You could last for weeks in the desert with just water."

"There's not an ounce of fat on me," he boasted. "As you'll soon know from hands-on experience," he added slyly.

Kate chose to ignore his comment and walked stiffly across the parking lot to his truck. Her body was tingling from just the thought of touching him. What would happen if she actually let herself go?

She couldn't decide if she wanted to know or not. Of course, according to him she would have no choice in the matter, so why worry about it? If she wanted to be in on the investigation, that meant being by his side, and that in turn meant putting up with his constant teasing.

"So be it," she muttered to herself.

"Excuse me?"

"I said, let's go eat."

* * *

The Mexican restaurant was cozy, and they sat at a booth in a dark corner secluded by tall plants. Kate wondered if Matt had tipped the hostess. It was the perfect setting for one of his seduction scenes.

"How did you discover this place?" Matt asked as they finished their meal.

"Friends. I came down with Paul occasionally, and we enjoyed eating here."

He glanced at her, pleased by the way she spoke so naturally of her late husband. The last thing he wanted was to try to compete with a dead man. "The last bite," he offered.

"No, thank you," she said fervently. "I can't believe we actually ate everything."

"There's still dessert," he reminded her as the waiter cleared their table.

Kate shuddered at the thought. "Go right ahead, I'm finished."

"I'll wait for you," he said, sliding closer to her. "When will you be ready?"

"Not today," she told him with an innocent smile, though she knew he wasn't talking about food any longer.

Throughout the meal Matt had managed to touch her often. Right now his hand was on her jean-clad thigh, his fingers gently caressing the soft white denim, warming her flesh beneath and giving double meaning to his words.

"Tonight?"

At a snail's pace he was working his way up to the top of her leg, the strong muscles beneath his fingers contracting with his roving touch. Kate calmly lifted his disturbing hand and dropped it between his legs. It was time to change the subject.

"Were you an only child?"

"Why would you think that?"

"Matthew Gage, can't you ever answer a direct question?"

"Sometimes." He smiled and slid his hand along the curve of her hip, up under her white and teal nubbly-yarn top. "It depends on the question."

Her low V neck had taunted him throughout dinner, giving him tantalizing glimpses of milky white skin contrasting with the soft honey-gold outline of her tan. Her smooth, warm skin felt like silk to his fingertips.

Kate grabbed hold of his wrist and flung his hand away from her, then turned her back on him, thoroughly disgusted. The man was a master at not giving out information, and despite the kind of response his body could evoke from hers, she wasn't about to get involved with a man she knew so little about.

Matt knew when to give in. He sensed that her stubborn resolve to find out more about him would stop any further progress in their relationship until he confessed all. Well, maybe not all. That would probably send her screaming into the night. He picked up the frosted stein of beer and slid it across her bare arm.

Kate whirled around to face him. "What the—"

He interrupted her before she really got wound up. "What do you want to know?"

Surprise flickered across her face as his words sank in. "Start with the last question. Were you an only child?" she asked quickly, before he could change his mind.

"No, I have two younger sisters, both happily married with families of their own. My parents are living in Tacoma, Washington, right now, but also have a place in Phoenix. My grandparents, both sides, live in Sun City, happily retired and enjoying life." He cocked his head toward her. "Did I leave anything out?"

"Have you been married?"

"Who says I'm not married now?"

Shock, like an electric current, ran through her. She continued to stare at him in disbelief. "Are you?" she asked, lowering her voice to a dangerous tone.

"Nope," he replied cheerfully. He picked up his glass and drank the last of his beer.

"You're lucky that's all gone."

"That's what I thought. I was betting you wouldn't throw the glass at me, just the beer."

"You're right this time, but don't count on it next time." Damn, he had nerve. *Too much nerve.*

He placed the glass far out of her reach. "I like my women unpredictable."

Kate again struggled with her temper. Was she just another female in a long line? She felt like a mass of jumbled rope. He had her so tied up in knots that between her raging hormones on one side and her brain saying slow down on the other she didn't know what to do. Slapping him soundly came to mind, but common sense prevailed. It wasn't possible to embarrass him and she knew it, but she could certainly embarrass herself.

"Cat got your tongue?"

Kate glared at him. "You should be so lucky." Quickly she composed herself and asked another question. "How did you get started doing whatever it is you do?"

Matt stretched out comfortably in the booth, his legs entangling with hers before he answered her question. "I started out pretty much like your husband did but with another company. I lasted about three years. Back then I was just learning the ropes, and every day was something new, for a while." He slid his arm back along the leather seat to rest lightly on her shoulder.

"What happened?"

"I got bored." His lightly callused fingers glided down the back of her neck and inside the edge of her top to caress her shoulder. "I'm a patient man, but even I have my limits. You'll see."

His fingers were becoming more daring and she felt the excitement his touch brought stirring in her. "G-go on."

"Gladly."

"I meant go on with the rest of the story, Matt."

He chuckled. "Oh, that. I quit and went to work for a private detective for a couple of years." His fingers were walking across the bare skin of her shoulders. "The challenge disappeared from that job as the firm became bigger and I encountered the same problems."

It was becoming more difficult to keep her mind on what he was saying. He was doing it again, seducing her anger away with just his touch. "What problems?"

"Too many bosses telling me how to do a job they couldn't do themselves." His fingers were tracing the delicate lines of her collarbone.

"And?"

"And what?" he asked huskily, slipping his hand down to cup one bare breast.

Her breathing became more ragged as the pad of his thumb moved back and forth across her erect nipple. The unspoken part of his restless career was obvious—the man liked to take risks.

"Matt?" she murmured.

"Yes?"

She could hear the approaching footsteps of their waiter on the tile floor. "You've got to stop, we're in a public place."

"Is that the only reason?"

She shook her head. "One of many."

He sighed loudly, then sat up straight, removing his hand before the waiter arrived to collect the check. He paid with the company credit card, grinning rather gleefully as he did so. Kate laughed in spite of the confused emotions coursing through her.

"Ready to go?"

Was she ever. "Yes."

The heat felt good as they stepped outside, an

awakening shock to her muddled system. The sinking sun painted a glorious, multicolored picture across the desert, hues of yellow and orange setting the sky ablaze with a bright red center resting on the distant horizon. The saguaro cacti were almost like statues, their long limbs resembling the arms and legs of someone lost and alone in the arid desert.

As they headed back to the hotel, Kate realized Matt still hadn't told her everything she wanted to know. "What did you do after the detective agency?"

Matt started to chuckle and the deep rumbling sound grew louder as he burst forth into open laughter. Kate sat in the corner of the truck, her arms crossed over her chest as she glared at him.

"What's so funny?"

"You are. You're as tenacious as a bulldog," he said, still chuckling quietly to himself.

"Must be the company I've been keeping," she shot back. "Now, answer the question."

He pulled into a parking space at the hotel and turned to face her, his arm sliding along the seat back behind her. "We could sit here close together in the truck, or," he coaxed, his fingers playing with her hair, "we could sit beside the pool and continue this discussion."

It was as if each strand of hair he touched conveyed his message through her body, a tingling sensation gathering at the center of her being and growing beyond her control. She had to get away from him and his touch. At least he had some decorum, and the pool was a public place.

"The pool. I'll meet you there as soon as I change," she said, almost falling out of the truck in her haste to get away from him.

"Hurry or I'll come looking for you." His words implied many things, especially if he found her beside the bed.

Kate struggled out of her clothes and into the one-piece bathing suit she wore in public, which successfully hid any flaws. Her skimpy suntanning suit, the one that had a top one size too small and made Kate feel busty, never made it out of her own backyard. With quick dexterity she twisted her hair up and clipped it into place. On her way out the door she grabbed a towel and her room key, then walked swiftly to the pool area.

As far as she could tell in the fading light, Matt wasn't anywhere in sight. She was carefully surveying the area for the best spot to sit when a hand skimmed across her buttocks, then settled, holding her womanly curves.

"What the—"

"Very nice," he whispered, squeezing her quickly before he let go. "I'll see you in the pool, I need to . . . uh . . . cool down."

In the wink of an eye he was in the water with a big splash. She could still feel the heat of his hand on her derriere. With leisurely movements Kate set her things down, then tested the water with her hand. Gradually she immersed her entire body in the water and began to swim. She needed to cool off too.

Matt swam beneath the water and surfaced beside her, keeping pace with her as she swam a few lengths. Together they left the pool and sat down at an umbrella-covered table, the outside lighting glowing around them. The night air was cool and refreshing after the heat of the day.

"Do you want something to drink?"

Kate leaned back, freed her hair, and squeezed out the excess water. "Maybe some iced tea or fruit juice?" She wanted all her wits about her tonight.

"Coming right up."

She was almost afraid to look at him, but she couldn't help herself. He was so big. Physical power emanated from him, and his muscular form was like a marble statue in motion. It hadn't been a boast; there didn't appear to be an ounce of spare fat on him. A sleek black bathing suit hugged his hips like a second skin. His chest tapered into lean hips, nice legs, his muscles clearly defined as he walked over to the poolside bar. Was he a runner?

As he turned to face her she realized that he wasn't a hairy man at all. His chest was covered lightly with varying shades of blond hair which trickled down to a single line and disappeared into his swimsuit.

She was still staring at him when he returned to stand in front of her. All his teasing seemed to catch up with her in a nerve-tingling realization. Such a man could indeed take her any time he wanted, but he was waiting for her, stalking her. Kate didn't know how much longer she could hold out.

Would he be gentle when the time came? The thought of all that strength and power unleashed on her in mindless passion was both terrifying and unbelievably seductive. He was right. Slowly but surely she was being drawn to him like a moth to a flame—or was it a fly to a spider's web?

"Orange juice," he said, handing her the plastic glass.

Kate had to clear her throat to speak. "Thank you," she murmured, startled by the effect his towering nearness had on her. She forced herself to think of something else.

Matt settled himself comfortably on a chaise longue and waited for the inquisition to begin anew. This lovely woman had more twists and turns than a snake. But he'd seen the desire in her eyes. He knew he'd see it again, too.

"Do you work alone?"

He smiled. Not a snake. A chameleon. She could change in the blink of an eye. "For the most part, yes."

"You do all the paperwork an insurance company requires by yourself?" she asked, her disbelief clear.

"No, I have two young women who do all that."

"How?"

"They've both been employed by insurance companies in the past and know the work. I dictate the reports, and they put them on paper."

She was curious. "How did you find them?"

"How does one find most women?" He quirked an eyebrow at her. She didn't look pleased. "I met the first one, Nancy, at Fidelity. She'd just given notice. She was determined to stay home with her baby for the first few years; I proposed she do my reports at home, and she agreed. Then Nancy found Rita for me, to fill the gaps she couldn't handle." He took a sip of tomato juice before continuing. "Then there's P.J., a college student who does book and computer research for me when I need it."

"And you do the exciting stuff?"

"Most of it's just routine digging. There are very few exciting cases. But insurance companies like to know these things beyond a shadow of a doubt." He finished his juice. "Shall we continue this discussion in my hot tub?"

He was already up and walking toward the pool gate without her. The choice was hers, follow him or no more information. Kate hesitated for a moment, then picked up her things and walked in his direction. If the situation was more than she could or wanted to handle she would simply get up and leave.

His room was a mirror image of hers, with the exception of the swirling, bubbling whirlpool off to one side in a tiled enclosure. She frowned. He looked like a satyr in a sylvan pond, beckoning to his next conquest.

"The water's ready, climb on in," he invited, easing his body deeper into the bubbling pool.

Kate slid in the opposite end of what looked like a giant, square, burnt-orange bathtub. The water felt heavenly on her tense body, easing her tight muscles. After a few minutes she realized that she'd be fast asleep in this warm cocoon if they didn't talk.

"How did you get started on your own?" Kate asked, her eyes closed.

"I knew a lot of people in the business and let them know I was willing to take any difficult cases they had," he explained lazily. "I'd earned a reputation for digging beyond where others had stopped, as well as the somewhat dubious honor of being considered a tough guy."

"You're that all right," Kate returned.

She was sprawled out, her eyes closed and lips parted invitingly. He cleared his throat. "Enough."

She felt his foot brush against her leg before he reached over and pulled her onto his lap astride his thighs. Her muscles felt so loose she couldn't object.

"Matt?" she murmured, looking at him intently.

"Kiss me."

Kate rested her hands on his shoulders and leaned toward him, tempted beyond reason. His mouth reached hers, claiming it gently, his kiss tentative, almost questioning. She felt the tip of his tongue licking her lips and opened her mouth to him. An almost inaudible groan came from deep inside him as his mouth settled firmly over hers.

She couldn't resist the temptation after all his recent teasing. Her hands slid down his ribs to encircle his waist, and she pressed her body closer to his.

Kate shuddered as his hands moved up from her hips to slide over her ribs, capturing her throbbing breasts. With practiced ease he slid his fingers under the straps of her swimsuit and lowered them down over her arms, baring her breasts to his sight.

"Lovely," he murmured, before taking one puckered nipple between his lips.

A hoarse, low whimper escaped her as he worked his magic on her trembling body. Moving from one to the other, he licked and kissed and worshiped her breasts. She could suddenly feel the heat of his masculinity pressing against the center of her desire, and the last few years of denial came crashing down on her.

She wanted him. But from somewhere deep within her, hesitation still whispered in her ear, a soft voice denying her need, speaking of realities and doubt. Was he too strong? Was she too vulnerable? Could this possibly be right?

Matt immediately felt the change, not a strong physical retreat at all, but a more subtle emotional withdrawal. She wasn't sure. For him, anything less than total willingness wouldn't do. He accepted that she wasn't ready to go any further. He might not sleep very well that night, but he accepted it. The choice was hers. He slipped her suit back up over her shoulders, arranging it properly.

"Kate?"

"Matt, I—I . . ." She looked straight into his emerald green eyes and saw his desire for her, along with his compassion.

He was quite a man, and it almost tipped the scales. But she wasn't ready yet and he would keep his word to wait until she was. She buried her face in his neck, needing his comfort and understanding. His arms enfolded her in his embrace and he held her close for as long as he could stand to, comforting her.

Then he stood up with her in his arms and strolled into the shower, where he turned on the water full blast—ice cold.

"Matt! Damn you!" Her shouted expletives were lost in the rushing water as he watched her scramble out of the tub and away from the freezing water.

"How could you?"

"I thought we'd save some time and water and take our cold showers together," he returned, pulling a towel off the rack and drying himself. "Sure cooled me down."

"You needed it," she snapped, wrapping her towel around her body. She was angry with herself, not him. Why was she plagued with these insane doubts? It wasn't like her to be so indecisive. "Dammit, Matt. What do you want from me?"

He tipped her chin up with one strong finger, forcing her to look at him. "Unconditional surrender, Kate." Softly, his lips caressed hers for a fleeting moment before he pulled away and swatted her on the rear. "Now, unless you plan on spending the night," he announced, ushering her toward the door, "you'd better get out of my room. And you wouldn't be allowed to get any sleep, either, I promise you."

"You and your promises," she muttered crossly as he walked her to her room. "How am I supposed to know which ones are real and which ones aren't?"

He opened her door and pushed her inside. "All my promises will be real before long. You are mine, sweet Kate, you just don't know it yet."

"I hope you have insomnia," she bit out through clenched teeth before slamming the door in his face.

"I probably will," he murmured, whistling as he returned to his room. She was weakening fast, and he could afford to wait. "But it will be worth it."

CHAPTER EIGHT

Chad Burch had been a successful executive for a major electronics corporation before a midlife crisis sent him chasing dreams of instant wealth in the Badlands; Chad had acquired gold fever. According to reports Kate's husband had gotten from the regulars at one of his favorite watering holes, he even claimed to be on the verge of a large precious-metal discovery.

His plane was old but in good mechanical condition, his record as a pilot long and spotless, the weather on the morning he departed for his glory crisp and clear. A few moments after takeoff, however, the FAA had another case of deadly wind shear to add to its extensive files, and the desert landscape had acquired a long, deep scar.

Chad might have walked away from the wreck if it hadn't been for the explosives crammed into the cabin of the light aircraft. As it was, there had been little left of the plane and only his dentures for his wife, Lenora, to claim.

"He was kind of young to have false teeth," Kate remarked as Matt and she rolled along a dipping, winding road on the north side of Tucson toward the Burch home.

"Gloria's husband was quite thorough in the report he made when he took over the case after Paul's death," Matt told her. "Evidently Chad Burch had a near-addiction to sweets of every description his whole life. I guess he'd never heard of brushing after every meal or dental floss."

Considering the situation they were in—and his failure to complete his planned seduction of Kate last night—Matt was in a remarkably good mood. She gazed at him, thinking about how close she had come to surrendering to him and knowing deep within that she would not escape the next time. He would be more persistent, and she wouldn't be able to resist.

With that thought she realized why the man had an infuriating smile on his lips. Matt had her right where he wanted her, within a hair's breadth of falling totally, passionately, under his masculine spell.

It was as he had promised; Kate wanted him to take her, was having a hard time thinking about anything else. She wanted to feel his strength and power within her, to at last allow herself to be swept into an oblivious ecstasy she knew would be greater than any she had experienced before. She was lost and she knew it. His next touch, his next kiss, would be her undoing.

"I hope that look on your face means what I think it means," he said, interrupting her thoughts.

Unsuccessfully fighting the color rising to her cheeks, Kate turned away and said crossly, "I was just enjoying the sunshine. You'd better watch that ego of yours or it'll pop the top off of this truck."

"I'll open the sunroof."

Laughing sensuously, he did so with one hand while steering the truck around another sharp bend in the road. Kate stared out the side window and sank into what he decided was a very appealing sulk. Soon, he thought—very soon—she would be his.

Matt hoped the busy signal he had gotten every time he tried to call Lenora Burch that morning meant she was home. It could be her daughter, Stacy, tying up the phone. From the report he'd read she was a somewhat eccentric young woman he didn't have any particular desire to talk to. If Lenora was out he would have little choice but to wait for her return, however, and the thought of making small talk with an eighteen-year-old environmentalist didn't thrill him.

Still, offspring sometimes had a penchant for discussing their parents' darkest secrets, so the effort might be necessary. Along with the more obvious aim of getting her into his bed, he had brought Kate with him on this trip for precisely that reason: she would be an excellent buffer between him and Chad Burch's feminine survivors.

"Nice house," Kate said, abandoning her sulk for the time being as they pulled up in front of the Burch residence.

"With the settlement she got from Fidelity she

can afford it." He got out of the truck and came around to give Kate a hand. She pushed him away and climbed out by herself. "Touchy, touchy," he said, chuckling.

Kate studiously ignored him and admired the yard. It was landscaped with more varieties of cacti than she had known existed; a bit overzealous in her opinion, but more natural than trying to force grass to grow in this climate.

When Matt strode up to the front door and knocked, she followed, trying to keep her gaze from lingering on the way his blue jeans molded to his lean buttocks and hips. The white short-sleeved knit shirt he was wearing accentuated his tan and powerful build. She was thankful when the door opened and gave her something else to focus on.

"Yeah?" the young man standing in the doorway asked.

He was the exact opposite of Matt. Clad in nothing more than jogging shorts, the youth was short and painfully thin, with an unnaturally pale complexion. His vacant stare indicated he was also high—on something other than the glorious, sunny day.

"We'd like to speak with Lenora Burch, please," Matt said politely, though he looked at the boy with distaste.

"Not here."

He started to close the door. Matt pushed it back open with one finger. "Stacy Burch, then."

"Stacy's at work." He tried to shut the door again, his face clouding when the simple pressure of Matt's finger kept him from budging it more than an eighth of an inch. "Come on, mister," he whined. "I'm on the phone."

"Must be a thrilling conversation," Matt muttered.

Kate stepped forward, seeing that Matt was losing his patience. "We really need to speak with them. Could you tell us when they'll be back?"

"Why?" The youth peered at her, blinking his glazed eyes against the bright sun. "What's this all about?"

"Listen, you little—"

"It's a personal matter regarding Stacy's father," Kate interrupted, shouldering Matt aside. "Nothing serious. But we'd appreciate it if you could tell us when they'll be home or where we might reach them." She gave him a pleasant smile.

Matt turned and stalked off the porch, muttering under his breath. The young man became more talkative once he was alone with Kate and her more gentle approach.

"He's dead. Stacy's father I mean."

"We know."

"And her mother doesn't really live here anymore, or at least not so you'd notice."

"Oh, really?"

He nodded. "Stacy gets a check once a month from her to keep the house up and pay her college tuition, but I haven't been able to get a job for a while, so she still has to work at the museum to keep us in—" He broke off, suddenly realizing what he was doing. "I really have to get back to the phone now."

"Could we talk to Stacy at the museum?" Kate asked quickly.

The young man shrugged. "Sure. It's the Arizona–Sonora Desert Museum, out near Old Tucson. She takes care of the animals and talks to the visitors—gives lectures and stuff. Stacy's real smart."

If this was her boyfriend, Kate had doubts about that. But she smiled and thanked him, then joined Matt. He looked at her, his lips pursed in irritation, but she also saw a hint of grudging admiration in his eyes.

"You appear to have handled that fairly well," he said.

"Fairly well? The way you were going he wouldn't have told us a thing."

"So you saved the day," he shot back sarcastically. "Quit preening and tell me what he said."

Nose in the air, she got into the truck and glared at him through the open window. "Not until you admit you couldn't have done that without me—and say it like you mean it."

Glaring back at her, Matt went around to the driver's side and got in beside her, slamming his door. "Don't push your luck. I would have gotten it out of him eventually."

"Is brute force your answer to everything?"

"Not everything," he replied, his eyes gleaming. "As you well know, dear."

Kate's face reddened. "For your information,

he told me more voluntarily than you ever would have gotten with threats."

"Do tell," he coaxed.

"Say it."

Matt sighed. "All right. You provided me with a valuable service back there," he said honestly. "You kept him talking when all I wanted to do was wring his scrawny little neck." He took her hand, squeezed it, and added in a soft voice, "Thank you, Kate. I'm glad you're here."

"That's more like it."

His sincerity gave her pause. She wasn't sure yet, but she thought she was actually beginning to convince him he needed her help. She hoped so, because now more than ever she wanted to see this investigation through, even though she knew what would happen if they did stay together.

"I'd love to know what's causing that delightful smile you're wearing," Matt murmured, "but first things first. Tell me what the kid said."

"How does it feel to have the shoe on the other foot?"

"Kate . . ."

It gave her great pleasure to laugh at his ferocious expression. "The most interesting bit of information was that Lenora Burch apparently no longer lives there."

"What?"

"She sends checks to Stacy to cover housing and a college education. Stacy works at a nearby museum to pay for incidentals—such as keeping her boyfriend from the horrors of manual labor, I presume."

"Curious method of parenting, but hardly unheard of, I suppose. Still, it makes me wonder where Lenora has gone."

"He didn't say. Probably doesn't know and doesn't care, as long as the checks keep coming and Stacy brings all her pay home."

"Where do the checks come from?"

Kate shrugged. "I think we'll have to ask Stacy about that."

"He told you where she was?"

"Like I said," Kate replied haughtily, "he was a regular chatterbox—once you left us alone."

"Keep it up, funny girl." Matt wagged a warning finger at her. "You'll pay for this later," he promised with a wicked smile.

No doubt she would. Her pulse quickened at the thought of the culmination of their mutual desire, knowing they were moving toward it at dizzying speed. One thing she could depend on with Matt—he kept his promises.

"Stacy's at the Desert Museum," she told him, trying to look unconcerned by his sensuous threat. "Head back to town and turn west on Speedway."

Matt started the truck and took off. "Yes, ma'am."

"Cut the sarcasm and drive. The later it gets the hotter it is out there."

It was already quite warm when they pulled into the parking lot of the museum. Featuring the flora and fauna of the Sonoran Desert region, it was actually more of a zoological garden than a museum in the traditional sense.

And yet it wasn't a zoo, either. The living animals and plants were displayed in natural settings, as close to those of their life in the wild as possible. Beavers and otters played in ponds and babbling streams. Puma lolled in the shade of their mountainlike habitat, while smaller predatory felines, such as bobcats, roamed lifelike grottoes.

Kate could see where Stacy Burch had gotten the idea for her front-yard cactus garden: such varied landscaping with desert plants covered the site. Samples of precious minerals like those her father had prospected for were displayed at the end of a stroll through a man-made cave, its dark, cool interior a pleasant break from the heat of the Sonoran daylight.

Though Matt wanted to hurry along, Kate put her foot down and got to watch the coatis—raccoonlike creatures with long, fluffy tails—as they carefully sorted through their food, eating all the grapes first.

They found Stacy near the aviary, recognizing her from the description the gatekeeper had given them. She was a pretty young woman, trim and lively, her curly black hair bouncing around her face as she spoke to some visitors.

"Yes, the birds are quite happy here. They wouldn't reproduce otherwise. In fact, some are just guests, brought to us with injuries. If they mend sufficiently they'll be returned to the wild, as will some of the young birds and animals born here."

When the visitors wandered off, Kate and Matt

approached her. She smiled at them as she bent down to rearrange some fruit she was putting out for the birds.

"Questions?" she asked helpfully.

"Hi, Stacy," Kate said before Matt could open his mouth. "My name is Kate Asher, and this is Matthew Gage. We'd like to speak with you about your mother for a moment if we may."

Stacy stood up, her friendly smile gone. She looked at them warily. "You with the cops?" she asked.

"Why would you assume that?" Matt wanted to know.

"You look like a cop," Stacy said, glaring at him with unconcealed animosity.

Kate chuckled. "No, Stacy, we're not with the police. Matt is working for Fidelity Insurance, the company that carried your father's life insurance policy." From the look on the young woman's face, that wasn't much better than a policeman in her opinion. "I'm . . . I'm his assistant."

Matt looked at Kate with one eyebrow raised, then turned his attention back to Stacy. "Is there any reason your mother would be in trouble with the law?" he asked her.

"If you're not a cop, I don't have to talk to you," she informed him, her chin thrust forward defiantly. "Enjoy the rest of the museum."

As she turned to leave, Kate put her hand on Stacy's shoulder. "You don't have to talk to us, but we wish you would. We need your help, Stacy. We're trying to track down some people, dangerous people, who have done some terrible things."

"You're not going to take away the money, are you?" Stacy asked, turning back to face Kate with desperate eyes.

Kate looked at Matt. "That depends on what we find out," he replied. His face remained expressionless. "Look, Stacy. I can't make any promises. But I can tell you that it's in your best interest to cooperate with me. If there is something illegal going on and you withhold information, thereby hindering investigation, you could be viewed as an accessory."

"You sound like a cop too," Stacy shot back. But her defiance had fled.

"Come on, Stacy," Kate said soothingly, taking her arm and leading her to a nearby bench. "Let's have a seat. And don't mind Matt," she added, giving him a withering glare. "He had a disappointing night and is taking it out on everybody."

Matt made a choking sound but kept his mouth shut, seeing that once again Kate's honeyed approach was likely to bring about better results. His admiration for her was growing by leaps and bounds. He joined them on the bench and let her take the lead.

"All we really want to know is where your mother is, Stacy. We went to your house, and the young man there told us she doesn't live there anymore. Is that true?"

Her eyes narrowed. "Tony's a jerk. I should dump him, I know, but . . ." She trailed off and looked at Kate, seeking feminine understanding. "He's just so helpless, you know? I just can't."

"I know." Kate patted her on the back, looking pointedly at Matt. "Men are strange beasts—insensitive clods most of the time—but they're the best we've got, so we have to make do." Matt glared back and motioned for her to get on with it. "I'll get back to Tony in a minute. Tell us about Lenora."

"Mommy dear?" Stacy asked sarcastically. "Tony shouldn't have said anything, but he was telling the truth. She doesn't really live there anymore. She's supposedly on vacation, but I haven't even talked to her in over a year, and then it was just a long-distance phone call. Not that it matters to me. I don't know where she is and I don't care. We were never what you'd call a close family. We just put up with each other."

"You're father too?"

She nodded. "I don't think I was exactly a planned child. Mother and he considered me a stone around their necks and didn't try very hard to hide the way they felt. When he hit forty and freaked out, I could see the writing on the wall. One way or another I was going to be on my own soon and that was fine with me."

"Then he crashed his plane," Matt prompted.

"Right. It sounds ugly, but it was really the best thing that could have happened, at least for mother and me. She got to travel like she's always wanted, and I don't have to worry about tuition or a place to live while I finish school. I'll get my degree in a couple of years and then I'm gone." She smiled in anticipation. "Besides, things were getting even weirder than usual around the house."

"In what way?" Kate asked, looking at Matt with raised eyebrows.

"They were both acting strange. They had always fought about money, but all of a sudden the fights stopped. My father kept talking about the big score he was going to make. You know, a gold mine or something."

"Or something," Matt muttered thoughtfully.

"Anyway, I guess he found a gold mine after all, though not the way he planned. What's this all about, anyway? I mean, the guy was insured to the hilt and he bought the farm. The insurance company paid off and that's that, right?" She looked at Matt hopefully.

"We don't know what's going on, Stacy, so we really can't say what's going to happen," Kate interjected before Matt had a chance to add to the young woman's worries. "Can you give us any idea at all where your mother might be?"

Stacy shrugged. "I get a check once a month from this bank in Acapulco. Mother's signature but some kind of holding company account, so I don't know if that's where she is or just where she keeps her money."

"It's a start," Matt said with a sigh. "Do you remember the name of the bank, its address, and the name of the holding company?" She nodded and Kate handed her a pen and notebook from her purse. "Now, getting back to the beginning of this conversation," he continued. "Why did you think the police would be coming to ask about Lenora?"

Stacy looked at her feet. "I guess I had this feeling something wasn't right," she admitted. "She made a big show at the funeral, but his death didn't seem to bother her like I thought it would."

"What are you saying?"

"You figure it out," she replied. "The moment the cash arrives she does this scene on how she's going on vacation to recuperate and disappears like a shot. I get money from Mexico, to keep up appearances and maybe to assuage some feelings of guilt on her part."

"You think she had something to do with his death?" Kate asked, her eyes wide with shock. Stacy nodded.

Matt was frowning. "Interesting theory," he muttered to himself. Then he looked at the young woman and smiled. "Thanks, Stacy. You've given us a lot of help and we appreciate it. Come on, Kate." He took her arm and started pulling her away.

Kate held her ground. "Just a minute!" She retrieved her arm from his grasp and went back to Stacy's side. "I know its none of my business, Stacy, but since I'm notorious for sticking my nose in where it doesn't belong, I'm going to give you some advice anyway."

"It's about Tony, isn't it?" she asked in a glum voice.

"Yes. You're a smart young woman, Stacy. You're pretty, you have a goal in life, and you're perfectly capable of attaining that goal no matter what happens in this mess with the insurance."

"You think so?"

"I know so. But take my advice. If Tony doesn't clean up his act, dump him like a hot potato. If he's not helping you he's hurting you, and you don't need any more hindrances in your life."

Stacy smiled. "Do you have any children, Kate?"

"Well, no, I—"

"Too bad. You'd make a great mother. Take it from somebody who knows firsthand what a bad one is like."

Kate leaned over and hugged her. "Good luck, Stacy."

"You too," she said slyly, looking over her shoulder at Matt as he waited impatiently in the background.

"Oh." Spots of color appeared on Kate's cheekbones. "I'm just his assistant," she lied.

Stacy shook her head. "I'm smart, remember? I don't envy you, though. Can you imagine how big that guy's babies are going to be?"

Matt seemed lost in thought on the way back to Phoenix, frowning away the miles and saying very little. Finally, Kate had had enough of his silence.

"Say something!" she exclaimed angrily.

"What?"

"Anything!"

"You're beautiful when you're hysterical," he offered.

Kate jabbed him in the ribs with her finger. "You know what I mean. I want to know what's going on in that methodical mind of yours."

"All right." He didn't want her to know it, but she had been invaluable to him on this trip. The least he could do in way of thanks would be to talk it over with her. "I've been playing with all the little pieces to this puzzle, trying to see what kind of picture I can make."

"And?"

"How did Stacy Burch's revelations strike you?"

"You mean that her mother might have had her father killed?" Kate shivered. "Horrible."

Matt nodded. "And then some. But it fits. Both Paul and David Tynly were working on cases where no body was recovered. If a body can't be examined, there is no way of knowing whether the deceased met his end in the accident or was murdered beforehand."

"True. And if in the course of their investigations Paul and David uncovered a murder-for-hire scheme, that could certainly have gotten them killed."

"Most definitely," Matt agreed. "In fact, it would fit the killers' modus operandi. They would be good at arranging accidents."

Kate frowned uncertainly. "And yet they broke their pattern, didn't they? Paul and David . . ."

"I know," Matt interjected, sharing her

doubts. "No attempt was made to make their bodies disappear. That piece doesn't fit."

"It would be even harder to avoid suspicion that way, wouldn't it?" Kate asked.

Matt nodded. "In some ways at least. Killing somebody and making it look like an accident would be more difficult than carefully fixing up an accident where no evidence of foul play was left behind, including a body. More planning would be necessary, but the victim wouldn't be alive to spoil those plans by surviving the accident."

"And here's another piece that doesn't fit," Kate said, preferring not to think about the kind of people who could do such a thing. "If this is a murder-for-hire scheme where a beneficiary has someone killed for the insurance money, why would Lenora Burch take the risk? I mean, Chad Burch was supposedly about to discover the mother lode."

"Stacy said they fought a lot. Maybe she just didn't like the guy."

Kate shook her head. "All she would have to do is wait until he got the gold or whatever, hire a good lawyer, divorce him, and stick him for a whopping settlement."

"Unless she knew all his talk about making a big score was just so much hot air," Matt pointed out.

"But Stacy said they suddenly stopped fighting about money," she reminded him. "Why would they do that unless their ship really was about to come in?"

"I don't have all the answers, Kate," Matt said irritably. "But I'm going to get them. We'll need every last one of them if we expect to solve this."

Kate smiled secretively. He had said *we.* Could it be that he was at last considering her a partner instead of an interloper? "At least we've got one good lead, right?" she asked, careful not to sound smug.

"The bank in Mexico?" He sighed. "Maybe it is and maybe it isn't. First I want to nose around in Florida, check out the particulars of the case David Tynly was working on."

"Oh, good. I've never been to Florida."

Matt took his eyes from the road long enough to give her a stern glare. "You're not going now, either," he informed her.

"But—"

"I'm grateful for the help you've given me, Kate, but your involvement stops as of now," he interrupted firmly. "I'm paid to take risks, you're not. There's a good chance this discreet inquiry will get extremely dangerous. The bad guys have seen us together, probably know that you were with me in Tucson and might even be following us now, for that matter. I doubt they'll care if you're an innocent bystander or not, and I can assure you that the closer I get to finding them, the harder they're going to try to stop me."

The thought made the hair on the back of Kate's neck stand up. But she wasn't about to let him dump her like a sack of potatoes, not after all she'd been through thus far. Besides, what he said made sense and it frightened her. She wanted to be with him more than ever now.

"If that's the case," she argued, "then don't you owe it to me to take me along? If these people might consider me a loose end that needs tying, I'll be safer with you than without you."

Matt chuckled. "Nice try, dear, but I'm way ahead of you. I'm not going to throw you to the snakes. You're going to stay at my place while I'm gone."

"I am not!"

"The matter isn't open for discussion, Kate. Your house is very nice, but as a secure place to keep you while I finish this, it isn't worth the brick from which its made."

"You make it sound like you're putting me under protective custody," she returned suspiciously.

"That's precisely what I'm doing."

Kate stared out the window in silence for a while. She wanted to be with him, and was honest enough with herself to admit that most of her reasons had little to do with safety, or even finishing out the investigation.

There were emotions simmering inside her she was much more afraid of than any gang of evildoers. Kate was getting to know this large, intelligent, extremely masculine man. And the more she saw the more she liked. In truth, the fear that really gripped her heart was the fear of what the future would bring. When this was all over, would he simply say thank you and leave?

Not that it was a matter of being used and

abandoned. She had had her eyes wide open concerning Matt's sensuality and its effect on her from the beginning. It seemed inevitable they would become lovers. But what would happen then? When she finally lost the battle against desire, would she lose her heart as well?

Pushing aside such disturbing thoughts, Kate took a final stab at convincing him to take her along. "I still think I'd be safer with you. What's so special about your place?"

"My security system for one thing," he replied. "It's about as good as you can get without armed guards and electric fences. And of course, there's Sonja."

Kate's heart skipped a beat. "S-Sonja?" she stuttered, fearing the worst. While he had been seducing her, had there been a live-in lover waiting for him at home?

"Beautiful and deadly. The best protection and most charming companion a man could have."

"Oh." Her heart sank.

Matt laughed. "We'll have to discuss that jealous reaction when I get back from Florida."

"Jealous? Me?" She sniffed disdainfully. "You wish."

"Sonja is my dog, Kate. She's a little of this, a little of that, rather a lot of wolf too, if the guy in Alaska who gave her to me was telling the truth," he explained, still chuckling. "He probably was. She's mellow with me and my friends but vicious with unwanted company, utterly fearless."

"Peachy."

"You'll get along fine. After all, there's a lot of wolf in me and you like me, don't you?"

"Not at the moment, no," she replied vindictively.

Matt reached over and caressed her cheek. When he spoke, the softness of his voice surprised her. "I know how you feel, Kate. I want to be with you, too. But this is for the best." His eyes took on a familiar sensual gleam. "And just think how glad I'll be to see you when I get back."

With that statement hanging between them, they drove along, Kate fuming silently but trying to enjoy the scenery. Traffic was so light as to be almost nonexistent. The few cars they did see were driven by people who evidently knew the route quite well from the way they raced by, obviously annoyed by Matt's refusal to go more than ten miles per hour over the posted limit.

A white semi pulled up behind them, seemingly content with Matt's speed for a moment or two. Then it steadily began creeping closer. Matt frowned.

"I thought I told you to buckle that seat belt," he said, his gaze alternating between the barren road in front of him and the view of the immense grill of the truck in his rearview mirror.

"Sorry." She clicked it loudly. "There."

"Come on," Matt muttered. "If you want to pass, pass."

Kate sized the situation up. "He can see farther than you can. Maybe there's a car coming the other way."

"Maybe." He looked in his rearview mirror

again. The semi had dropped back slightly. "Uh-oh," he said ominously.

"What?"

"Brace yourself."

She glared at him. "What are you going to do? Cause another wreck?" she asked sarcastically. "I'll tell you what I think. I think you're paranoid, that's what I—"

The last of Kate's sentence was lost when the semi rammed the back of Matt's truck, bouncing the whole vehicle forward with a protesting screech of the tires. Matt fought the wheel as it wrenched in his hands, trying to keep the truck going in a straight line.

"He's crazy!" Kate cried out in disbelief. "We could have been killed!"

"I think that's the whole idea, dear," Matt said through clenched teeth. "Hold tight!"

The semi hit them again, much harder, as if the driver had just been getting a feel for it the first time. Matt's truck was big compared to a car, but compared to the behemoth vehicle behind them it was a toy. The force of the collision made it skew sideways, Matt's lightning quick reactions the only thing between them and disaster.

Kate closed her eyes, fear pumping through her veins like a living force. This was what it must have been like for Paul. A more powerful car, ambushing him in the middle of nowhere at night, the sound of metal hitting metal and then the ditch coming up at horrible speed.

Matt started weaving back and forth on the road, but it only made his truck less stable, and when the semi came at them once more he narrowly escaped getting hit in the side. He tried to speed up. The powerful diesel engine of the semi throbbed in their ears and it caught them easily.

"He's playing with us!" Matt exclaimed in outrage. Kate groaned, terrified beyond words.

Then the driver's intent became distressingly clear. He increased his speed, making it impossible for Matt to hit the brakes lest they be crushed beneath the giant's wheels. Yet another dry wash loomed directly in front of them, the sound of the semi's engine like a death rattle close behind. As they went around the corner he was going to shoot them into the rocky bank like a billiard ball into a pocket.

Matt did the only thing he could: he got mad. "Grab something and hold on!" he yelled above the screaming of the semi's engine.

Kate barely heard him. Her eyes opened wide as she saw Matt pull hard on the steering wheel, veering the truck away from the tractor trailer rig on their tail. She saw the side of the road approaching as if in slow motion, felt her mouth open to form a scream that wouldn't come. A gnarled mesquite tree vanished under the truck with an explosive crunch, followed by a stand of jumping cactus, the truck bouncing violently underneath her. She felt the seat belt as it dug painfully into her waist and shoulder, keeping her from flying forward as they slid and bucked to a stop beside an ancient saguaro.

The truck engine died. Back on the highway the sound of the semi trailed off into the distance, a mocking toot of its air horn reaching her, then fading to silence. Kate tried to swallow, but her mouth was bone dry, and her face was as pale as a sheet. She looked at Matt.

"When I said grab something," he announced with a grimace, pulling her fingernails out of his thigh, "I didn't mean my leg."

"Sorry," she croaked.

He sighed heavily and rested his chin on his chest. "What was that you said about me being paranoid?"

Kate looked at him. "Forget it."

"Thank you. Are you willing to stay at my place now?"

"Yes!"

CHAPTER NINE

A pair of pale blue eyes watched Kate as she settled more comfortably on the chaise beside Matt's pool. Waiting patiently, silently, hidden and unseen, the watcher stayed perfectly still until Kate had drifted off to sleep again beneath the hypnotic rays of the sun.

Only then did the quiet observer move forward. She held her weapon proudly at the ready in front of her, aiming for the warm flesh of Kate's back, so obligingly displayed by the bikini she wore. Closer, closer she crept without a sound. When she was practically on top of Kate she paused for a moment, then thrust her weapon home.

Kate's bloodcurdling scream filled the quiet afternoon air. "Ooh! Sonja! You're nose is like ice!"

The dog's arctic blue eyes seemed to laugh back at Kate as if she enjoyed the reaction her assault had brought about. Dipping her head, she happily lapped up the remainder of Kate's iced tea, gave Kate's shoulder another poke with her nose for good measure, then tried to stuff her great bulk beneath the chaise.

"You silly goose!" Kate cried, holding on with both hands as the chaise bucked and bounced across the concrete skirting of the pool. "You won't fit under there. Go find some other shade to sleep in."

Shady or not, Sonja next decided that the best place to be was in Kate's lap. It was absurd, of course: the dog was immense. When they were standing side by side, Sonja almost came up to Kate's waist. Kate pushed her off, but as a consolation prize she showered the dog with the kind of rough-and-tumble attention she seemed to prefer, grabbing handfuls of her silver gray fur and rubbing vigorously.

"I know, girl. I miss him too."

As if in reply, Sonja whined. She looked at her new friend almost sympathetically, tongue lolling at the side of her mouth, then padded across the deck on feet the size of saucers to seek a cooler spot to await her master's return.

Matt had been gone for two days. He had said he wouldn't call unless he needed to talk any new discoveries over with her. He hadn't called, so she didn't know whether that meant he hadn't found out anything or didn't need her.

So, feeling rather useless and abandoned, Kate settled into a routine of sleeping, raiding his well-stocked larder, and taking care of Sonja. She had also spent a good deal of time lazing by his pool, an elongated rectangle made for swimming laps.

Perched on a hill overlooking the city, looking like a layout in an avant-garde architectural magazine, his house was everything he had said it was and then some. It was comfortable, it was designed for convenient living, and it virtually bristled with security devices.

Though she acted like an overgrown puppy, Sonja was as described too. Like her lupine ancestors she spent most of the day dozing, most of the night patrolling her territory. She even had her own door, one that opened only to her, thanks to some kind of electronic device hidden in her collar.

Evidently the collar also caused the various detection devices to recognize her as a friend—she came and went past the security barrier as she pleased. One look at her great head and powerful, fang-studded jaws was enough to convince Kate that a friend under Sonja's protection was as safe as a baby in its mother's arms.

Still, Kate's sleep had been fitful the last two nights. She was worried about Matt, herself, and the tenuous relationship building between them, as well as about this confusing investigation. It didn't help matters any that she felt like a prisoner, even if her cell was very comfortable and plush.

She sighed sleepily and decided to try to take a nap before fixing another lonely dinner. Under Sonja's watchful gaze she got up and went into the house, deliciously cool after the constant Phoenix sunshine. A quick shower made her feel even more relaxed, and she practically collapsed on the bed in the guest room, not even bothering to pull the sheets over her naked form. She was soon fast asleep.

She awoke to the sound of soft breathing next to her ear. Something warm and wet glided down her bare spine as she lay sprawled on her stomach amid the rumpled sheets.

"Go away, Sonja," she mumbled, flailing one arm in a sleepy attempt to push the beast away.

Her hand touched something hairy. But it wasn't Sonja's soft fur. Kate gasped and her eyes popped open when she realized what was happening. Matt had crawled into bed with her, and her hand had tangled briefly with his thick blond hair.

"You're back," she whispered softly, looking at him over her shoulder, her face partially buried in the sheets.

"Still very observant, I see." His sensuous green eyes were drinking their fill of her beauty.

The sight of his large, bronzed, masculine body, though partially hidden to her gaze by the rumpled sheets, was more than enough to trigger her sleepy senses into action.

"I dreamed of you," he whispered, not touching her, letting his eyes caress her first, waiting for her to wake up. His touch would soon follow, bringing her body awake as well. He wanted her so badly he ached. "Did you dream of me?"

Kate looked into his eyes, the hypnotic fire burning in them slowly seducing her toward him. Unconsciously she raised herself on both elbows and swayed a little in his direction.

"Yes, I did," she replied in a whisper, surprised by the huskiness in her voice. She had dreamed of him every night since he left. The dreams came flooding into her mind, like a warm caress across her thoughts.

"Erotic dreams?" he asked, stretching out beside her on the bed, his feet dangling off the end.

His head was resting in the palm of his hand as he braced himself on his side. One knee was drawn up comfortably toward her, but not touching her. He looked into her eyes, smiling slightly, watching the slow transformation as she awakened from her nap. He could see the realization in her eyes, relished the way her breathing quickened. She knew what he wanted. The time for waiting was over.

Moistening her lips, Kate opened her mouth to speak but this time no words came. Her breath made raspy little sounds in her throat as she anticipated what was to come. The pulse in her neck was already beating at a frantic pace and he hadn't even touched her yet.

But the tingling in her spine reminded her that he had stroked her, tasted her with his tongue to awaken her. How could she have forgotten so quickly? Her heart beat faster and faster, the tingling between her thighs a sweet ache waiting to be filled.

"Those must have been some dreams," he murmured as a soft pink glow enveloped her face.

Kate looked away from him, letting her dark auburn hair swing forward to hide her emotions, suddenly unsure of herself. The only other man she had ever made love to was her husband. And some of the things she'd dreamed of doing with

Matt she had never even thought of trying with Paul.

His large warm hand began gently stroking her back, slipping over and around the angled curves of her shoulder blades. "Relax. We have all the time in the world."

"Matt, I—I'm . . ." Her voice trailed off, and she bit her lip, not sure how to put her doubts into words. She wanted him, wanted to please herself and him, and yet . . .

"What lovely blades you have, my dear," he mumbled against her back, nibbling on them.

"What?"

"Tasty too," he murmured, continuing to nibble his way down her back, his teeth nipping at the tender skin on her sides.

Kate tried to wiggle out of his grasp as he toyed with her ribs. "Stop that, you beast. It tickles."

"Mmm. Ticklish," he said, in a voice reminiscent of a mad scientist. "I'll save that information for another time. Right now I think I'm feeling a bit too serious."

"Matt . . ." His tongue was leaving a moist trail across her hips, gliding down the full curves to her buttocks. She shivered with delight.

"What a lovely derriere," he murmured, leaning across her lower back and resting on his elbow, trapping her beneath his side, the warmth of his body blending with hers. "Just my size," he added, grasping the moon-shaped orbs in his hands and squeezing them gently, then gliding his hands down the silky skin of her legs. With gentle firmness he grasped the inside of her thighs and pushed them apart.

Kate writhed beneath the onslaught of his caresses, trying to free herself from his trap and his tantalizing touch. Arching her back she again tried to slip away from him, breathless from his touch.

"I'm getting to that part," he teased, tightening his grasp on her. "Patience, sweet Kate." Leaning down, his tongue skimmed along the backs of her legs, his hands and body holding her still beneath his touch.

"Matt!"

"No? You don't like that?" he whispered, continuing to stroke her quivering body.

"Yes, but—"

"Oh. You want more." His fingers were caressing her intimately, teasing her with the power he held over her.

"Let me go!"

"Am I hurting you?"

"I don't know!" she cried out.

"I'll kiss it and make it better."

"No!" The implied taunt sent liquid fire racing through her veins, the fire pooling within her, weakening her crumbling defenses. "I don't think—"

"Oh. I'll wait, then," he agreed, not wanting to frighten her. Reaching down he grasped one foot and nibbled on her bright red painted toes.

"Matthew, stop that, I have sensitive feet," she yelped, trying to free her foot from his grasp.

"You have sensitive everything, and I've only just begun," he informed her.

Kate groaned into the pillow, gasping for breath, her mind and body reeling from the shock of his ardent touch. But Matt wasn't about to let her cool down. He casually rose and picked her up to turn her over, his strength such that she felt like a rag doll in his arms. She pushed damp tendrils of her hair away from her eyes and looked up to find him towering over her. Her eyes widened.

He was so big. In a lot of ways he still frightened her; that dangerous element in his character never seemed to completely leave him. His strength and size could overcome her anytime, and yet for some strange reason that ability intrigued her, excited her. He could be so gentle, but would he be gentle now?

"What—what are you doing?"

"Gazing at your beauty," he murmured, then sat down on the bed, his hands slipping down her legs to encircle her slender ankles. With a gentle tug he pulled her toward him, placing her legs to each side of him.

Kate reached up to touch him but he stopped her. "Your turn will come," he teased, kissing the back of her hand and then her fingers, one by one, sucking each one in turn before setting her hand on the bed above her head, far away from his body.

The simple gesture shot waves of desire through her, and she grabbed hold of him as he continued his exploration, writhing beneath his touch.

"Patience," he teased. "I don't want you jumping to any conclusions now. Will you never learn the joys of being methodical?"

His hands smoothed their way across her stomach and up over her rib cage. For the first time she felt the partial weight of his body on hers as he stretched out over her. His hands cupped her breasts, caressing them to his will.

Kate looked up into his warm green eyes, compelled on by the desire she saw there. She let go of the sheet she had been clutching with her other hand and ran her fingers through his thick blond hair as he pressed wet kisses around the tanned edge of each breast, working in a circle to the center. His tongue gently flicked each puckered nipple in turn, before he settled on one. With a soft suckling he coaxed the tip back to softness. Tiny kisses rained across her chest as he headed for his next conquest.

Her fingers slipped through his hair and down to his shoulders of their own volition. She gasped softly as he worked his way up the almost transparent skin of her throat, the hair on his chest caressing her trembling pink breasts.

"Such a stubborn jaw," he whispered, "covered with such gorgeous skin." With his lips he committed to memory her face, curving around her cheekbones, across her brow to her ears. His tongue traced the curve of her ear, dipping inside suddenly.

"Matthew!" She was astonished by the bolt of

desire that shot through her at that caress. She could feel it deep within her, a hot molten desire trying to escape.

"Yes?" His voice was low and husky, emotion filling every nuance. "I'm listening."

"I—I want—"

He chuckled sensuously. "You see? I promised you I'd make you want me."

"Now," she whispered, gently raking her fingernails across his smooth back.

"You little hellcat." A deep shudder raced through his already aroused body.

"Let me make a promise of my own," she crooned, pushing him off of her when he allowed it. "It won't hurt a bit."

Kate sat up quickly and assumed a superior position. He really was a rather large man, not just tall, but big. Delicate fingers skimmed over him, feeling each and every ridge of his back, flitting over the curves of his arms to his firm legs. She could feel his impatience with her, but she continued to thrill and tease, knowing she would pay for her deviltry. A low moan and another deep shudder rippled through his body, bringing great pleasure to her. She smiled down at him, an almost evil light gleaming in her eyes. Who had the power now? It delighted her to realize that she could control him too, at least this way.

"Kate!"

"Yes, dear?" she asked innocently as he moved out of her tantalizing grasp.

"You witch," he murmured as her blue eyes laughed at him openly. "Your time has come."

He lowered his mouth to hers, his tongue plunging deeply into the hot moist cavern awaiting him. With gentle hands he positioned her beneath him. She could feel his heat and throbbing hardness pressing against her, making her shudder, her fingernails digging into his sides now that the moment had arrived.

"You're not backing out now, Kate." He held her firmly in place. His husky, passion-filled voice reinforced his words; he would not be denied.

Kate rolled her head slowly from side to side, not looking at him, not sure of what she wanted. Still some small part of her was frightened, of the unknown, of him.

"Yes, Kate," he whispered softly, coaxing her gently. "Speak to me, tell me what's wrong."

"Matt, I . . ." She paused, then tried to speak again. "It's your s-size," she realized. "I don't think . . ." She was babbling, thoughts no longer coherent in her passion-filled mind. Her fingers, obeying a will of their own, circled his waist, kneading the bronzed skin rhythmically.

"Shh. You'll be fine. I wouldn't hurt you for the world, sweet Kate."

He covered her lips with his own, his tongue plunging deep inside her mouth as he slowly filled her. Matt wanted it all, he craved her with a longing quite new to him. The warmth of him flowed into her, bringing once-forgotten feelings raging through her. It had been so long, so very, very long. She cried out in joyous rediscovery.

"Matt—Matthew. Oh yes!"

"Are you sure?"

"Damn you, Matthew Gage," she gasped, "don't you dare tease me now!"

"You want me?"

"Yes, I want you," she yelled, tormented beyond belief.

"Then you'll have me, Kate."

Together they moved in a furious rhythm, simmering desires too long denied boiling out of control. It was as Kate had thought it would be, powerful, buffeting, riding the hurricane of passion they had been keeping bottled up.

To her great surprise, however, she was his match—or at least this time he was allowing her to think so. Her need was so great that her own strength and size seemed well able to contain his searing desire. They rushed headlong toward the culmination he had promised, a desperate, clinging madness such as she had never known before. The madness lingered, past the brink and beyond, on and on until even Matt's seemingly endless strength could barely keep pace with Kate's breathless demands.

At last she sprawled beside him, their legs intertwined, her head resting on the curve of his chest. She could feel the rapid beat of his heart beneath her ear, hear the brisk pulse begin its slow descent with each breath he took. She smiled a secret smile. It was a good thing it was Matt who had seduced her; a lesser man might not have survived.

Matt held her securely in his arms, still reeling from the harmonious blending of their bodies. Now more than ever he was determined to keep her safe. She had given herself to him and he intended to keep her. Her face, nuzzled in his neck, was hidden from his view. He'd just have to guess what she was feeling. As for himself, he felt he had found the woman of his dreams.

"It's been a long time for you, Kate."

"You noticed," she mumbled into his chest, tickling his skin. She hadn't dealt with this kind of honesty before, but there wasn't any reason to let him know that. Sheer bravado was the only way to go. "Not that it's any of your business."

With whispered soft caresses he stroked her body. "It is now. I think you just answered a lot of questions about yourself."

"Beast! You think you know everything," she raged, pummeling his body with her fists.

Matt quickly flipped her onto her back and towered over her. "I know I've got you where I want you."

"That's what you think. I'm too hungry."

He pinned her to the bed, nibbling on her neck. "Me too."

"I demand to be fed!" she cried, pushing against his chest. "If I lose weight, you'd break me in two."

"Since you put it that way . . ."

"I'll also faint from hunger," she threatened, her body going lax beneath him.

"Play fair."

"I will." She batted her blue eyes at him coquettishly. "Later." Much later. She needed some time to let what had just happened sink in.

His voice rumbled with emotion. "You witch.

Be warned. Just like you, I hold people to their promises."

Working in companionable silence amid the afterglow of their lovemaking, Matt and Kate prepared a Mexican feast together in his modern kitchen. As they worked they fed each other bites of rich cheese and shared a glass or two of fruit-filled sangria. Passion still smoldered beneath the surface, showing in their eyes and the knowing looks they exchanged.

There would be more ecstatic delight this evening, but first they had to eat, and as they ate, they talked. Sonja kept an eye on the proceedings, obviously hoping a morsel or two would find its way to the floor. She waited patiently, alert to every movement.

"As you know," Matt said as they sat peacefully enjoying the restorative meal, "Bob Hale, the man in Florida who was swept into an underwater cave never to be seen again, was something of an adventurer, a man with a passion for diving in dangerous waters to explore shipwrecks."

Kate nodded, sipping her wine, reluctant to return to business. By the gleam that lingered in Matt's eyes she knew this discussion wouldn't last long. She didn't have any idea what tomorrow would bring, but for now they were together and she was intent on enjoying every moment.

"I remember reading something to that effect in David Tynly's report," she replied.

"Did you get as far as his beneficiary?"

"I assumed it was his wife."

"Nope."

"Then who?"

Matt grinned. "Not who," he said, his eyebrows raised dramatically. "What. The dear departed left all his worldly goods—namely a whopping chunk of Fidelity cash—to an obscure oceanographic research foundation."

"Curious," she commented, "but commendable I suppose. I mean, if he didn't want his wife to get it he could have taken it with him or something weird like that."

"That's the interesting part. In a way, Bob Hale *did* take it with him, or at least made sure that the insurance money would further his own interests. Guess who set up the foundation in the first place?"

"Him?"

"Exactly."

Kate shrugged. "So? A lot of people do that sort of thing, at least the more philanthropic ones. Trust funds, grants, scholarships."

"True. But they don't usually name their mistresses to head them up, do they?"

"Not unless she happens to be a lawyer or something," Kate pointed out. "Or in the case of Bob Hale's foundation, an oceanographer whose research he admired—along with her more earthy assets," she added with a sly grin.

Matt chuckled along with her. "Well, she's neither a lawyer nor an oceanographer, or much of anything else as far as I could tell. That's what took me so long down there. Digging up information on the foundation and her proved difficult. I had to hang around with some of Hale's diving buddies to get most of it."

"Why didn't you just go to the foundation?"

Matt's grin grew even broader. "Because it isn't located in Florida. It isn't even located in the United States."

"Acapulco?" Kate asked, leaning forward excitedly.

"The Caribbean, actually. Cayman Islands."

She frowned. "Oh."

"The bank handling the funds is in Acapulco."

"You rat!" Kate tossed her napkin at him. Sonja jumped, saw that it was only a piece of cloth, and sighed impatiently. "The same one?" Kate asked. He nodded. "Then we have a link, don't we?"

"We do indeed," Matt agreed, raising his glass.

Kate touched her wine glass to his, joining in his triumph, but a moment later she frowned in puzzlement. "But we still don't really know what's going on, do we?"

"No, but we're getting closer," Matt said. "The checks Stacy's mother sends her come from Acapulco, the same bank handles the money for Bob Hale's foundation, and the south-of-the-border location ties in with where we think the people behind this might have their base."

"We may have the where, but we still need the who, what, and why," she pointed out.

Matt shook his head. "We already know why, Kate. Money. It's the force behind most criminal behavior. There's a lot of cash changing hands and you can bet the bad guys are getting their share," he explained. "Hopefully this lead on the bank is going to take us to them."

"That still leaves what."

"I know. The murder-for-hire theory has a few flaws in it, but it's still the only thing that makes sense. Bob Hale sets up a foundation, which apparently functions mainly as a retirement plan for his mistress. To remain in her good graces, so to speak, he shows her his insurance policy naming her the beneficiary."

"I see," Kate interjected. "It's a nice gesture, but there's always the chance that he'll suffer a pang of remorse near the end and leave it to the wife instead."

Matt nodded. "Right. So the mistress, deciding she likes the idea of being rich enough to spend the rest of her days studying seashells, helps Mother Nature along and has good old Bob killed."

"Enter our expert accident arrangers again," Kate said thoughtfully. "You're right, it fits. But . . ."

"Don't tell me you're going to punch my brilliant deductions full of holes again?" Matt asked, slumping in his chair with a sigh.

Kate ignored his theatrics. "Forgetting for a moment that it looked like the Burches were going to come into money and that she could have gotten her share using less extreme means, Lenora Burch at least had more motive."

"How so?"

"She was in her midforties. Maybe she decided that getting the insurance money while she was still young enough to enjoy it was worth the risk of having her husband killed," Kate said. "But I assume Hale's mistress was younger. He was only thirty-seven if I remember correctly."

"Yes. She's in her late twenties according to Hale's former diving buddies."

"Well then. Here's a woman—young, presumably good-looking—with her whole life ahead of her. Granted it would be nice to live it in comfort, but would it be worth the risk of having a man killed to accomplish that? Especially when he engaged in dangerous sports and there was a fair chance he was going to leave her well off soon anyway?"

"I hate it when you're logical," Matt grumbled.

Kate chuckled. "Still, you were right when you said it's the only scheme that makes any sense, I suppose. Until we get down there and dig around, we're only second-guessing ourselves into a quandary."

Matt hummed thoughtfully. Then he realized what she had said and looked at her in amazement. "We already settled this, remember? You're not going anywhere. Acapulco may very well be the lion's den, Kate. I'm not taking you with me."

Kate gave him a long, hard stare, then got up from the table, going over to the broad expanse of glass overlooking the city lights spreading into the distance. She had known this was coming, and had had plenty of time to think about what to say. Saying it, however, especially after the intimate evening they had shared, wasn't going to be easy.

She sighed. "Matt, I'm tired of having this argument."

"So am I," he said softly, getting up and joining her at the window. "There are a great many things I'd rather do right now than fight."

"Me too." She glanced at him briefly, then returned her gaze to the lights. "But I'm going, and that's final."

"Kate—"

"I mean it, Matt," she interrupted, pulling away from his tempting, coaxing touch. "You know you'll need me. The places you'll be going to ask questions won't be on the tour lines. You'll need somebody who speaks Spanish. And if you end up going to the Caribbean, a smattering of French here and there wouldn't hurt."

Matt cleared his throat irritably. She had a point and he knew it, but he wasn't giving in. "It's too dangerous."

"I'm going to see this through, Matt," she warned him. "With or without you."

Spinning her around to face him, he searched her face, so angry with her he wanted to shake her. There was something in her eyes, the same determined resolve he'd seen the night he caught her prowling around the Fidelity building.

"What's that supposed to mean?"

"You can't hold me here. This place is good at keeping people out, not in. If you leave without me I'll just follow you." She wondered where she got the courage in the face of his fury. "I started this, Matt. My suspicions, my badgering at Fidelity—it all started with me. And I'm going to be there at the finish whether you like it or not."

He didn't doubt for a minute that she would do as she said. What really bothered him was that look in her eyes. She wanted to be there at the finish, all right, but would she be there looking for truth—or vengeance?

"Damn it, Kate! Can't you see I don't want you in danger? Can't you see I—"

She put a finger to his lips, almost afraid of what he might have been going to say. "I don't want you in danger either, Matt," she said softly. "But you will be, and I want to be with you." She pressed herself against him, willing all the powerful emotions whirling within her to reach out and touch him too. "Don't you want me?"

This wasn't fair. He did want her. The thought of being away from her filled him with anguish. "You know I do," he replied.

"Then take me with you."

"I can't." But he knew he was fighting a losing battle and she seemed to sense his indecision, pressing her point home.

"Yes, you can. What's more, you know I'll go without you if you don't," she told him seriously.

"Damn! You'd do it, too, wouldn't you?"

She nodded. "You can't very well tie me up."

Sighing, Matt wrapped his arms around her and laughed ruefully. "Don't tempt me," he said, kissing the tip of her nose.

Maybe it was for the best. He had the feeling they were walking into danger, and his feelings on such matters were seldom wrong. But he also had the feeling that if she did follow him, if he weren't there to keep an eye on her, Kate might do something she would regret the rest of her life —providing she could get close enough to the people they wanted without getting herself killed first.

For all the gentleness she was capable of, Kate also possessed an amazing inner strength. She wouldn't be the first person to take the law into her own hands in the pursuit of justice. It was called revenge, and he knew her well enough now to know that some small voice inside her cried out for it, to put her late husband's memory to rest if nothing else.

Matt wanted this final remnant of Paul's memory out of the way too. He was hesitant to put a name to the feelings he had for her, but now that he had shared her lovemaking, he knew he never wanted to let her go. So she would come with him, and they would exorcise the darkness within her together.

"All right," he said softly. "If you come with me, at least I can protect you." And protect her from herself, he added silently. "But only if you'll do what I say, follow my every instruction to the letter."

"Everything," she promised.

He grinned. "Everything?"

"You really are a contemptible beast!" she exclaimed, trying to push him away. She yelped with surprised pleasure when he swept her into his arms and carried her through the house. "Where are we going?"

"To bed, dear. We have an early plane to catch tomorrow."

"Oh." She sighed happily and rested her head against his broad chest, knowing full well that they probably weren't going to get any sleep at all. "Whatever you say, Matt. See how good I can be?"

"Mmm," he whispered, putting her down on his bed and covering her body with his own. "Show me."

"They are together again, at the Sky Harbor, waiting for the plane to Acapulco."

Static crackled across the miles of telephone line linking Carson with his Phoenix henchman. Nevertheless, Carson could tell by Angelo's voice that he was puzzled. It was understandable. Carson was rather bewildered by the situation himself, though he would naturally never admit it.

Asher's widow had been the only one intelligent enough to realize that her husband's death hadn't been an accident. As expected, however, no one had listened to her. When Fidelity lost two men in as many years, though, the sleeping giant awoke and hired a top gun. This, too, was as expected. Gage decided to question the woman. Fine. She accompanied him to see the widow of the other man. Again it made sense.

From there it got very confusing. First he took her to Tucson with him, a move that would have cost him dearly had not Angelo underestimated how good a driver Gage was. Carson decided that the woman was more valuable than he had thought. Perhaps they were even a team.

But then Gage left her behind at that fortress of a house with the evil, watchful dog. If they were a team, why didn't she accompany him to Florida as she had to Tucson? Suspecting a trap of some kind, Carson had decided to pull back and watch for a while.

It had been a mistake. Gage was proving as good as his reputation, getting closer in two days than the others had in two weeks. Surely he must realize that now was the time to take every precaution. A man like him would sense the danger increasing.

So what does he do? Collects the woman and heads for Acapulco as if going on holiday. Why would Gage risk the woman's life in this manner?

"Do you think they are lovers, Angelo?" Carson asked.

"Who can tell? They sit very close together."

Carson swore under his breath. "Let them come," he said at last. "It is apparent they wish to perish together as well."

CHAPTER TEN

Almost immediately upon arriving in Acapulco, it became obvious to Matt that Kate was going to be indispensable—even if she had blackmailed him into letting her come. She had been there before, he had not. She spoke the language, he did not. When she initiated a lively discussion with a cab driver at the airport, he realized that the cab had no meter and the price of a ride to their hotel was negotiable.

Matt was a sophisticated man in a great number of ways. This was hardly the first time he'd set foot off American soil. It had been a few years since he'd traveled abroad, however, and it took him longer than he expected to shift mental gears. This was another country. He was a foreigner.

Kate was too, but she'd made the attempt to bridge the gap by learning the language. She was going to save him a lot of time.

"I didn't bother telling Dale that you were coming with me," Matt said as they settled into the back seat of the cab for the trip to their lodgings, "but I have the feeling he's not going to mind a bit."

"No?"

"No. You're going to save him a mint in cab fare alone. And I had this vision of myself using sign language to wrangle a list of depositors out of the bank manager, who would be laughing hysterically because he spoke perfect English."

Kate grinned. "You just have to know how to talk to them," she said, then turned her attention to the scenery flashing by, as much to keep the driver honest as to enjoy the view.

Tourism had begun in Acapulco as early as the thirties. Along with the sun, beaches, and warm water that had always been there came the action and excitement that drew millions of visitors each year. There was no place in Mexico like it, or anywhere else for that matter. Acapulco was one of a kind, and it was little wonder the resort became the jewel of the jet set.

Like Kate's native Phoenix, the place naturally had its share of growing pains. The rapid influx of fun seekers, the building of places to house them, and the development of a tourist industry to attend to their every need brought intense growth. Acapulco was a city, after all, and like all cities had its share of sharp contrasts. There were rich and poor, successful and unemployed, opulent and dingy, all set against the natural contrast of mountains meeting the sea.

And of course, Kate thought as they rolled along the boulevard hugging the bay, it was Mexico. Rich in history, thrilling, vaguely dangerous even when one wasn't tracking down a group of killers. With Matt at her side, however, she wasn't afraid. She reached out and took his hand. He squeezed it reassuringly.

They checked into their hotel—Matt went first-class with his expense account; the hotel was practically a self-contained city in itself—then set off immediately in search of the bank. And immediately ran into their first snag.

"That's it?" Kate asked, looking askance at the tiny pink building tucked into the middle of the block.

"Hardly what I had expected either, in view of the cash that's supposedly channeled through the place," Matt agreed.

A few minutes talking with the so-called bank manager was all it took to convince them they had made an error. The place was obviously little more than a mailing address, probably set up to serve a number of obscure operations such as the holding company that sent Stacy Burch checks from her mother every month. In other words, their hot lead was a dead end.

Trudging down the street, they found a restaurant that smelled delicious despite its somewhat dubious appearance and realized they were ravenous. They ate, cooling themselves off afterward with potent Mexican beer. Clouds scudded across the sky above their sidewalk table, announcing the rainy season's usual afternoon shower.

"You look surprisingly happy, considering the blank wall we just hit," Kate commented suspiciously. "What kind of plan are you formulating now?"

"A siesta I think," Matt replied, grinning. "See? I know some Spanish."

"Very good. Now tell me—"

"The flight and this heat have me feeling like a wet noodle," he interrupted lazily, stretching his arms over his head and yawning.

Kate yawned too in spite of herself. "Sounds good, but what do we do after that?"

"I have an idea or two." The gleam in his eyes told her exactly what was on his mind.

"Matt!"

"We'll follow our leads."

"What leads? That guy couldn't—or wouldn't—tell us a thing."

"True. But this might," he replied, pulling a folded sheet of paper from his shirt pocket.

Kate watched, her eyes wide, as he spread it out on the table. It appeared to be a list of names and addresses of the people who did business with the so-called bank. She looked up at him in amazement.

"I didn't see you get that!"

"Of course you didn't. You were too busy talking to the guy and he was too busy looking at your legs," Matt explained. "I just slipped into his files and appropriated this list."

"I see I've underestimated how sneaky you can be."

Matt shrugged and leaned back to look at her legs. "No, you just underestimate how much thigh that dress shows when you sit down and cross your legs."

"So what does it say?" she asked impatiently, poking him in the ribs to get his attention.

He laughed. "Well, to begin with, Lenora Burch does live here, or at least there's a current address listed for her. After we rest we'll go see if she's home."

"Really?" Kate looked at the list where he pointed. She whistled in surprise. "Nice location."

"You can find it, then?" Matt asked. Kate nodded. "Good. The second interesting thing is the number of holding companies and such on this list. They all shuttle funds through that little rerouting center we visited, and they all show a marked preference for tax-free offshore banking." He looked at her expectantly. "Suggest anything to you?"

Kate frowned. "Offshore . . . The Cayman Islands?"

"Bingo. Which is, incidentally, the location of the phony oceanographic foundation run by the late Bob Hale's mistress. After we have a chat with Lenora, we'll head over there and see what we can dig up." He looked at her, his expression suddenly as cloudy as the sky overhead. "We're getting close, Kate. I can feel it. Are you sure you won't—"

"Reconsider and go back home?" she finished for him, anger shoving its way into her tone. "No. We're in this together until the bitter end, Matt."

He sighed. "All right. But I wish you wouldn't put it quite that way." An ominous rumble followed his words, then the first drops of rain. "We'd better get out of here."

To their utter amazement they managed to get a cab, a situation that made Kate drop any attempt to haggle over the price. As they drove along the glistening streets she glanced over at Matt. He was frowning thoughtfully.

"I know that look," she said, wary of the plot he was probably hatching. "What now?"

"I was just thinking. Lenora might be more forthcoming if she doesn't know who we are. It would be better if we could somehow arrange to meet her socially." He grinned at Kate. "You know, just me and the little woman down here on vacation, glad to meet you, Lenora."

Kate knew he was suggesting a bit of playacting, but her heart still skipped a beat at the thought of being Matt's wife even in jest. She turned her face away for a moment until her nerves stopped jangling.

"There might be a way," she said at last, turning back to him. "The place Lenora's staying is kind of like a community, seclusive to be sure but interconnected. If we were to become a part of it we might arrange an introduction."

"Are you suggesting we set up housekeeping?" he teased.

She had to work hard to meet his eyes. "It's a resort facility. I stayed there once when I won a contest Fidelity held. I made a friend there who should be able to get us in, especially this time of year."

"A man or a woman?"

"Excuse me?"

Matt's eyes had narrowed slightly. "This friend of yours. Is it a man or a woman?"

He was jealous! Kate let him stew for a moment, enjoying the possessiveness she could practically feel emanating from him. In a way, though, it frightened her too.

She had been denying the tender emotions building within her. Seeing him like this made them spring to the surface, and in view of the charade of posing as his wife she could easily get her foolish heart broken.

Still, Kate couldn't resist the urge to tease him in return. "A man," she said slyly. "And I don't really know him that well. We just had a summer . . ." She trailed off with a smile. "A summer acquaintance."

"Acquaintance," Matt muttered.

"It was before I was married," she explained.

"What?"

"He was so tan," she said in a dreamy voice, "so kind, so mature." She sighed and looked out the window at the rain.

Matt sat there fuming silently. It took him a moment to realize that her shoulders were shaking. What was she doing? Crying at the memory of a summer tryst?

"Now you listen to me," he said angrily, pulling her around to face him. She was laughing!

"We'll have to discuss that jealous reaction," she said in a syrupy tone.

"You . . . You . . ." Matt spluttered. He put his hand behind her neck and brought her lips to his, kissing her deeply, punishing her sensually with his tongue. "You're playing with fire, Kate. I warn you."

"He's seventy years old, Matt," she murmured, her lips swollen from his kiss.

"Seventy!"

"I said he was mature, didn't I?" she taunted, well aware she would pay for toying with him and feeling desire course through her at the thought. "I was too shy to even go out on the beach. He's practically a permanent fixture at the resort, the sage in residence in a way. We sat around on his patio and talked."

"That's all?"

"Yes." She chuckled throatily. "I'm sorry."

"You're not a bit sorry, you little . . ." He kissed her again, more gently this time, his lips lingering on hers. "Just wait till I get you back to the room."

The cab driver, who had been enjoying the show immensely, made some comment in Spanish. The words may have been strange, but Matt didn't miss the inflection.

"What did he say?"

"He said his wife will be glad he picked us up. For some reason he feels the urge to go home early and see her."

* * *

The lingering rains pelted them with warm water as they raced into the hotel and hurried toward an empty elevator. Once inside Kate couldn't resist the opportunity. Scooping the rain water from her arms, she flung the droplets at him, laughing gleefully.

"Why you! Take that," he said, shaking his wet hair over her as the elevator opened up.

An older couple stood looking at them curiously, unsure whether to enter the elevator or not. Water trickled down the dark paneling, mute evidence of some kind of playful disturbance. The soggy combatants straightened up immediately, trying not to laugh.

"It's raining," Matt explained innocently.

"Going up?" Kate asked.

"We'll wait," the couple mumbled, smiling but backing away from Matt and Kate as if whatever it was might be catching.

They both broke into laughter when the doors slid shut again. It seemed to take forever to get to their room. Matt pulled her inside and locked the door behind her, growling at her like a bear.

"Come here, woman. I want you."

"Are you sure?" she teased, leaning away from him. Her fingers sprawled out over his shoulders, her only contact with his body.

Matt drew her away from the door and steadily closer to him. "I'm sure. This short dress you're wearing has been taunting me all morning."

"This little thing?" Kate whirled away from

him, the white sundress flashing up high on her thighs. She hadn't felt this good for quite a few years.

"It's almost indecent." He walked toward her retreating form. Her breasts actually seemed to strain against the cotton.

"Everything vital is covered," she objected throatily. "Or was."

Her nimble fingers released the first of many tiny buttons holding the front of her dress together. Matt's breath caught in his throat as she peeled back the bodice, revealing glimpses of white and honey-tanned skin to his smoldering gaze.

"Yes?" she asked throatily, dropping the bright yellow belt to the floor.

"Yes," he murmured, reaching out to draw her into his arms. She evaded his grasp with a ballet-like spin.

"Patience, remember," she taunted saucily, raising her arms over her head. With teasing motions she removed her hairpins one by one and dropped them to the floor. Dark auburn locks came tumbling down around her shoulders. "Slow and methodical, just like you."

"There are limits," he informed her, grabbing her hand and pulling her to him. "And you've just reached mine."

Matt felt the power of her movements ripple through him. With ease he held her in the crook of his arm, his other hand free to explore her at his leisure. Kate leaned back, tempting him, her throat freely disclosed to his touch. His gentle fingers slid down her cheek to cup her face in his hand, and his slightly callused thumb skimmed across her parched lips.

He could feel the warmth of her breath against his thumb, the misty air caressing him in a yearning way, her lips parted in welcoming invitation. It was as if time stood still, this moment frozen in their minds as they looked at one another, each savoring the gentle desire of the other.

With the tip of her tongue Kate tasted his callused thumb, strong white teeth gnawing on the skin. Matt shuddered with an aching need for her, that simple caress inflaming his desires even more. Slipping his hand around the back of her neck he pulled her toward him, his eyes never leaving hers.

Softly, tentatively, their lips met, both hesitant to go too fast lest they lose this growing tenderness between them. Again and again their lips met, growing bolder with each touch, each caress, the sensations coursing through them reaching fever pitch.

Suddenly Matt held her away from him, his chest heaving as he gasped for air. He wanted to make this time last, to stretch the moment out forever and ever. He forced his taut muscles to relax and with great difficulty slowed his breathing.

Kate was trembling in his arms, wanting this feeling of desire and almost desperate longing to last an eternity. With hands as shaky as an aspen leaf in a summer breeze, she began to unbutton his shirt, wanting to feel his flesh against hers.

Deft fingers slid the thin cotton garment from his shoulders, letting it fall at their feet.

"Wait," he murmured.

With quick, sure movements he released the tentative hold her dress had on her hips, watching as it floated down her legs to pool about her ankles. A pair of brief white panties were her only covering now. He started to pull her into his arms.

"No." She stilled his hands, then released his pants, drawing them down his strong thighs. "Equal terms," she murmured, gesturing for him to step out of the slacks.

Matt complied with her wish, his gaze encompassing the glossy smoothness of her back and the feminine curves of her slender waist. He liked the way her delicate white briefs were slipping down lower on her hips. His eyes blazed with anticipation.

Her soft hands caught the waistband of his shorts, then skimmed over his thighs and down to his feet, leaving him bare. She stood up gracefully, gazed at him with a haughty air, and promptly tripped over her own slip-on sandals.

"Gotcha!" He caught her around the waist, drawing her toward him. "Were you trying to escape, my beauty?" he asked, his tone of voice that of a pirate outraged by any hint of disobedience.

Kate slid her arms around his neck, her pliant body stroking him lightly, sensuously, enjoying the crisp feel of his hair against her breasts. "What do you think?"

He swung her up in his arms. "You're not going anywhere without me."

"I don't want to." Her arms stayed tight around his neck, and he sank down to the waiting bed with her in his arms.

Matt threaded his fingers through her hair, the velvety auburn tresses sliding softly from his grasp and onto the pristine white sheets. He buried his face in her throat, inhaling her soft womanly scent.

"Matthew," she whispered, cradling his face between her hands. "I need you."

"You'll have me soon," he promised.

Softly, reverently, he caressed her, again learning the ways of her body as it responded to his, casting aside the last barrier between them. His hands slipped over her hips and beyond, feeling for her readiness, glorying in what awaited him.

He took her gently, with great care, his desire to pleasure her to the limits of her endurance. He had yet to find the depth of her willingness; he had decided it was a quest on which he would gladly spend a lifetime.

"Matthew!"

"Yes, love?"

"Come with me."

Together they became one, a single entity, soaring high and bursting across the sunset into shattering pieces, still one. And yet again the smoldering embers ignited, the flames of their passion lifting them beyond peak after peak of shuddering joy. Breathless, limbs entangled and sprawled in disarray, they watched as the thunder clouds outside their window made patterns of light and shadow upon their damp, heated skin.

They lay side by side, silently absorbing the feel of each other, the communication of their shared warmth flowing between them as the rain gently spattered the windows. The pleasant, hypnotic sound of the summer storm brought them calm at last, lulling them to sleep, a tender cocoon of ecstasy surrounding them in a gentle glow.

Kate's friend did remember her. He was pleased to see her back there with a man, especially one who so obviously cared for her. After commenting on how lovely and glowing she looked—a comment that made her glow even more—he had a word with the manager and they were soon settling into a luxury bungalow carved into the hillside.

He didn't ask any questions as to why they wanted to find Lenora Burch. According to him she had become something of a flamboyant fixture at the resort herself, complete with a rather mysterious lover who shared her rooms. Armed with his description of her, Kate and Matt set out on their discreet search.

They found her playing tennis on one of the lighted courts reserved for resort guests. A soft sea breeze caressed them as they sat watching her play, drinks in hand and trying to behave like well-to-do newlyweds. It wasn't too difficult. Their intimacy was woven around them like a gossamer web, a magic any onlooker would find hard to miss.

Matt had made sure to get a table Lenora would have to walk past when she left the court. She was a good player, beating her opponent soundly by running her from net to baseline and back. The other woman walked off the court drenched in perspiration while Lenora was barely winded.

"You have very nice form," Matt said to her as she approached.

Kate hated her instantly for her athletic prowess and dark, svelte beauty. The fact that she looked at Matt like he was a rare steak didn't help any either.

"So do you," she said wryly, extending her hand to him with scarcely a glance at Kate. "I'm Lenora."

"Matt." They shook hands. "This is my wife, Kate."

Lenora nodded at her, still holding Matt's hand. "Pleased to meet you. Do you play?" she asked him with a broad smile that said she wasn't talking about tennis.

Matt smiled back. It was obvious Lenora was a woman who cared little about the social niceties, such as keeping her hands off another woman's husband. That would make the task of getting to know her much easier, with the side benefit of getting back at Kate for teasing him earlier.

"I have been known to dabble," he replied, winking at her. "I'm not on your level, though."

"You never know. Maybe I can test your mettle sometime."

When she finally let go of Matt's hand, Kate grabbed it and held it in her lap, wondering if she should count his fingers. If Lenora Burch took the bonds of matrimony so lightly, might she think just as little of breaking other boundaries as well?

I'm acting like a jealous wife, Kate thought. Just because Lenora was trying to be a husband thief didn't mean she could also be a husband killer.

"You must have just arrived," Lenora said.

"That's right," Kate replied, feeling the need to enter the conversation. "How did you know?"

"I would have noticed you before this otherwise." She was still looking at Matt.

"Just got here," Matt said. "We're a little at loose ends as a matter of fact." He raised one eyebrow slightly and added wryly, "You look like a woman who knows the ropes. Have any ideas on what to do this evening?"

Lenora nodded, a wicked grin on her tanned face. "I'm having a party tonight in my bungalow." She started walking away. "You can't miss it," she told them, glancing back over her shoulder. "Just follow the broken hearts."

"I think I'm going to throw up," Kate muttered.

Matt chuckled. "Well. That was easy enough."

"You'd better go change your clothes. I think she drooled all over you."

"Careful. Your baby blues are turning green."

"Stick it in your ear," Kate shot back, elbowing him in the ribs. She rolled her eyes and mimicked him. "You have very nice form."

"It got us an invitation. That's all that counts."

"Is it?"

Matt looked at her and laughed. "You don't seriously think I'm attracted to that walking barracuda, do you?" He put his arm around her and hugged her. "Don't worry, Mrs. Gage," he teased. "You're the only woman for me."

It was a joke, but it totally disarmed her. She smiled reluctantly and kissed him on the cheek. "Thanks. I needed that."

He pulled her to her feet. "Come on. Let's take a walk. Then we can come back and put on our party togs. What does one wear to a bungalow bash?"

"I'm going casual," she replied. "I suggest you wear a suit of armor."

Lenora's lodgings were much like Kate and Matt's, with the exception of a private pool. She must have made some wise investments with the money from her husband's life insurance. A paltry million wouldn't last long against two years of the life-style to which she had become accustomed.

Then again, Kate thought vindictively, maybe she was a prospector, like her husband had been. She certainly looked like a gold digger.

It wasn't a trail of broken hearts that had led them to her place, but a steady flow of people. It could be that Lenora was popular, but judging by the way the faces of the crowd constantly changed it was more likely she was simply a good bartender. She poured with a heavy hand.

"Matt, darling. Here. Have a martini," she insisted when he and Kate approached the carved teak and onyx bar. "You too . . . um . . ."

"Kate."

"Of course. How could I forget such a cute name?"

Matt held tightly to Kate's arm, preventing any retaliatory action. "Quite a party."

"Enjoy life to the fullest, that's my motto," Lenora said. Abdicating her drink-mixing throne, she came slinking around the bar and latched onto Matt's arm. "Come on, I'll give you a tour."

"That would be nice," Kate said.

Lenora shot her a cold look. "Be a dear and mix the drinks for a while, will you, Katie?"

Kate's eyes narrowed dangerously. "Why, you—"

Matt cut her off. "We won't be long, dear. I'm sure you'll find someone interesting to talk to."

She knew he meant Lenora's lover. "Oh."

"If I don't leave someone in charge of the booze these sots will cart it all off," Lenora added, tugging on Matt's arm impatiently.

Kate glared at her, then leaned close and whispered in Matt's ear. "Watch yourself. I'll be dusting for fingerprints later."

He grinned and allowed himself to be dragged toward the open patio doors. Kate sighed, then moved behind the bar. Maybe she'd get lucky.

After all, weren't people supposed to tell things to a bartender they would never tell anyone else?

She refilled a few glasses and chatted briefly with some of Lenora's guests. Most actually were what she was pretending to be, tourists on holiday. They were smiling, laughing, and generally having a good time. Except for one man in the corner of the plush living room.

Trying not to stare, Kate observed him curiously. Something about him didn't quite fit. He was more casually dressed than the others, an irritated expression on his face as he watched the people milling around him. It was almost as if he saw them as interlopers on his territory.

Lenora's lover? Kate felt a spark of excitement at the prospect of actually doing some detective work in Matt's absence. She caught the man's eye and he frowned, then started toward her. When he got close enough, Kate noticed a small white stick protruding incongruously from the corner of his mouth. He sat down on a stool in front of her, still frowning.

"Do I know you?" he asked, the stick in his mouth bobbing up and down.

"No, we just arrived today. I'm Kate Gage," she replied. "Lenora asked me to keep an eye on the bar."

He nodded. "I remember now. You came in with that big guy." He grabbed the end of the stick and pulled it out of his mouth. It was a red, well-chewed lollipop. "Your husband?"

"Yes. Lenora's giving him a tour of the house."

"Figures," he said bitterly.

He certainly sounded like a jealous lover. "You are . . ."

"Chuck."

"Can I fix you a drink, Chuck?"

"Might as well," he said, shrugging his shoulders. "It's my liquor, after all."

Bingo. "What would you like?"

"In the refrigerator there's some ice cream. Stick a scoop or two in the blender and add some Scotch. A couple of spoonfuls of sugar, too."

Trying not to make a face, Kate did as he asked, then watched in distaste as he downed the concoction. "Isn't that a bit sweet?" she asked politely.

"I like it sweet." He stuck the lollipop back into his mouth and smiled sarcastically. "I guess that's why I don't dump Lenora. She has such a saccharin personality."

Something tugged at a corner of Kate's mind, but she didn't get a chance to think about it long. A woman's scream spilled into the room from the patio, bringing a hush to the crowd. The scream came again, louder, and Lenora staggered into the room, her face white.

"Some man with a knife!" she cried. "He . . ." Lenora fainted and crumpled to the floor.

"Matt!" Kate made a dash for the patio, shoving people aside and almost tripping over Lenora as she reached the sliding glass doors. "Matt! Where are you?"

"Over here," came his muttered reply. He was standing at the edge of the patio, looking down at the beach. "Damn!"

She rushed over to him, throwing herself into his arms. He winced. "What happened? Are you . . ." Her voice trailed off in horror as she saw the blood smeared on the shoulder of his torn shirt. "You're hurt!"

"Just a scratch," he assured her. "This is getting annoying. Not only do they keep coming after me, but I keep letting them get away." He peered down at the beach, trying to see into the deep shadows. "It's no use. The guy must be part rabbit."

Tentatively at first, then in a murmuring rush, people flowed out to the patio and crowded around them, asking what happened and if Matt was all right.

"We don't need this attention," Matt whispered in Kate's ear. "It's okay, folks," he said to the crowd, his voice jovial. "Just one of my creditors. I'm fine."

More than willing to forget the incident and return to their party, the revelers laughed with him. Pulling Kate along by the hand, Matt went back into the bungalow, stepped over the still prone form of Lenora, and headed toward the door.

Chuck blocked their exit. "Shall I call the police?" he asked, looking hard at Matt.

Matt stared back. "I don't think Lenora needs the publicity." He didn't either, at least not yet.

"What's that supposed to mean?"

Kate stepped between them. "Matt, this is Chuck, Lenora's . . . um . . . house guest."

"House guest?" Chuck exclaimed incredulously.

"Nice to meet you," Matt said, pushing his way past him. "Give Lenora our thanks for a lovely evening. When she wakes up, that is."

"Yeah." He watched them hurry out the front door, his face a mask of suspicion. "I'll do that."

CHAPTER ELEVEN

Back in their own bungalow, Kate made Matt take off his shirt and stretch out on the bed. She practically had to sit on him while she cleaned the gash he had received from the attacker's knife. It wasn't as bad as it had first appeared, and he seemed much less concerned with the wound than his failure to catch the man.

"These guys are making a shambles of my reputation."

"Sit still!"

"It stings," he complained. "Besides, having you on top of me like this is giving me ideas."

"Behave yourself." Relief washed over her as he pulled her close and kissed her. He was fine. "You'll live. I don't know about me, though. I almost had a heart attack when Lenora screamed."

"It didn't do much for my heart either, I assure you."

"What happened?"

He grinned. "Are you sure you want to know?" She scowled at him. "Okay. Lenora had me practically bent over the patio railing—"

"Stop." She pulled away from him and sat on the edge of the bed, her arms crossed. "I want to know about the attack, not your moonlight escapades."

"That's what I was trying to tell you. Lenora pounced on me and—"

"Poor, defenseless baby!"

Matt sighed. "Will you listen? I was at the railing trying to escape her clutches when this guy took a swipe at me from behind. If Lenora hadn't chosen that moment to try and pull me into her arms he would have slit my throat instead of my shoulder."

"Oh." Kate shuddered and reclined beside him, holding him tight. "I thought for a moment that maybe she lured you over there—set you up for the kill so to speak."

"No. She lured me into the shadows all right, but murder was not her intention. And she practically split my eardrums screaming when she saw the knife." He flexed his shoulder gingerly. "Looks like our friends are getting nervous. No more accidents, just cut and run."

"Not funny."

"No. Interesting, though. It was a risky, almost desperate attack. Makes one think they didn't want me talking to Lenora."

"Did you?"

"Did I what?"

"Talk to her, you dreadful tease!" she replied, poking him gently in the ribs.

"Some. She wasn't in the mood to talk."

Kate took her head from his chest and looked

at him. "Did she seem suspicious? Like she knew who we were and why we're here?"

"Are you kidding? You saw her latch onto me. Did she look at all suspicious to you?"

"I guess not."

Matt shifted to his side so he could look at her. "Her house guest, on the other hand, didn't seem to like us at all," he remarked.

"I was getting on all right with him. It's you he doesn't like, and no wonder. Judging by his bitter reaction when I told him Lenora was giving you a tour, I get the feeling she's anything but a one-man woman."

"Hmm," Matt said thoughtfully. "It's odd. I had this strange feeling I'd seen him someplace before. Something about his eyes, I think."

"He was odd, all right. Had a lollipop in his mouth most of the time I was talking to him and had me mix him this awful Scotch milkshake. Said he liked sweets." She gasped. "Matt!"

He grimaced when she jostled his shoulder. "What?"

"Chad Burch liked sweets."

"So?"

"Don't you get it?" she asked excitedly.

Bouncing off the bed, she went to Matt's suitcase and pulled out a large manila envelope. Inside were the Fidelity case files. With his usual thoroughness, David Tynly had included a photograph of the insured, Chad Burch. After staring at it intently for a while she went back to the side of the bed and thrust the picture under Matt's nose.

Matt looked at it for a moment, then back at Kate, his lips pursed. He shook his head. "I hope you're not suggesting that Chad Burch and Chuck are one in the same?"

"That is exactly what I'm suggesting," she replied.

"I'll admit there are similarities. It would have taken extensive plastic surgery though. And there's a more plausible explanation in any case. You know as well as I do that women are often attracted to the same kind of man over and over again."

"Are they?" Kate looked at him pointedly. "You aren't anything like my late husband."

"I'm an insurance investigator."

She blinked, but quickly regained her footing. "Some investigator! You refuse to see the facts when they're right under your nose."

"You don't have any facts, Kate," he told her bluntly. "I'm willing to admit that Chuck's resemblance to Chad Burch is a pretty strange coincidence, one we should probably look into further, but—"

"But what? It fits, can't you see that? The clues don't really line up with a murder-for-hire scheme. Why would Lenora have her husband killed if he was about to come into money? She wouldn't. The big score he was talking about wasn't a gold mine, it was the insurance money from having himself declared dead."

Matt frowned. "Maybe, but—"

"And Bob Hale's young mistress," Kate continued, caught up in her own theory. "Why bother arranging to have him killed when his love of danger would probably kill him soon enough anyway? On the off chance he might decide to leave his money to his wife? Come on," she said with disgust. "I'll bet we find somebody who just happens to resemble Mr. Hale sharing her bed and the money he channeled into that phony oceanographic foundation."

"Would you let me get a word in edgewise?" Matt demanded. "You're grasping at straws, Kate. It's a poor detective who forces the clues to fit some wild supposition."

"It's no wilder than a murder-for-hire scheme, and it makes more sense," she told him angrily. Then she noticed the smile on his face. "Did you say clues?"

He nodded. "I told you before I don't trust coincidences any more than you do. It's sort of crazy, and it implies an amount of organization and planning that boggles the mind, but you might just be onto something, Kate."

"I am? I mean of course I am!"

Matt pulled her onto the bed with him and hugged her fiercely in spite of his wounded arm. "That's what I like, a woman with the courage to enforce her convictions," he said, kissing the tip of her nose. "Seriously, it bears checking out."

"Let's go!" She tried to pull away from him.

"Calm down," he warned softly, pulling her back into his arms. "I've had a long day, I'm tired, and my shoulder hurts. Besides, what do you propose we do? March over there and accuse them?"

"Yes."

Matt laughed. "If they are part of some conspiracy, don't you think that might be just the tiniest bit dangerous?"

"I guess," she sighed, realizing he was right.

"We'll have to have proof before we confront Lenora and Chuck."

"Chad," she corrected.

"Maybe," he retorted sternly. "And quite frankly, confronting them isn't really our—or rather my—job. The police will have to handle that part, no matter what scheme or conspiracy we uncover," Matt explained. "We need to check into it, go over to Grand Cayman and see if there really is a Bob Hale look-alike wandering around, and generally continue to make nuisances of ourselves until something gives."

"All right." Kate sighed and cuddled next to him, realizing that she really was quite sleepy. "Tomorrow."

Matt yawned. "Tomorrow."

They got ready for bed, then settled down in each other's arms, listening to the wind in the palms and the surf in the distance.

"Matt?"

"Hmm?" he replied sleepily.

"What kind of proof would we need? To convince the police that Chuck is Chad, I mean."

"Chuck's Chad," he mumbled back.

"Matt?"

"Fingerprints I suppose," he replied, barely awake. He yawned and pulled her closer. "We'll talk about it tomorrow. Go to sleep."

* * *

Kate's eyes popped open and she looked at the clock on the bedside table, its pale green numbers informing her it would be dawn soon. Matt was fast asleep beside her. She was glad he didn't snore. With the size of his chest the noise would probably reverberate her right out of bed.

She felt alert and rested, though she had had some trouble getting to sleep. Try as she might, Kate couldn't quit thinking about it. Okay, so maybe she was jumping to conclusions, and some pretty bizarre ones at that. But if Chuck was really Chad, wouldn't the incident at Lenora's last night have scared them?

If there was a conspiracy, presumably the organizers would have assured the clients they would take care of anybody who came snooping. It wouldn't do to have their clients running all over, jumping at shadows and attracting attention to themselves. Enter Matt, closing in on them and escaping their attempts to stop him.

They might run away and hide. They certainly had the resources. She and Matt would never get the proof they needed then. The more she thought about it, the more agitated she became. She slipped out of bed carefully so as not to wake Matt, certain he would stop her if he knew what she was up to.

He was a good man. A little too methodical perhaps, but just as capable and thorough as she had thought him to be the first time they met. Was he ever!

Matt had capably and thoroughly seduced her,

won her mind and body in his typically methodical fashion. It wasn't something she dared think about too much just yet, but he had won her heart, too. Looking back on it, it had been crazy for her to fight the desire she had felt the very first time he had touched her, kissed her. But if a fortune teller had informed her she would fall head over heels in love with a man like him, Kate would have broken the crystal ball.

Looking at him as she quickly and silently got dressed, feeling her heart swell with tenderness, she knew it was true. She was in love. But that still didn't mean she was going to follow his orders blindly.

The sun had not yet begun to climb above the horizon when she slipped out into the crisp, predawn air. She could smell the sea, hear the gulls as they wheeled overhead, probably on their way to one of the fish markets near the beach. The only people up and about were a couple of joggers, too intent on their pulse rates to notice Kate as she made her way to Lenora's bungalow.

She wasn't going to do anything foolish. The only plan she had was to make sure they were still there. It was eerily quiet in this section of the resort, probably because most of Lenora's neighbors had been at the party and hadn't gone to bed until very late. All but invisible in the gray light, Kate tiptoed around back and onto the patio, intending to peek through the sliding glass doors for any sign of Lenora and her so-called house guest.

When she saw that the remnants from the

party had not yet been cleared away, a thought occurred to her. They needed fingerprints to prove that Chad Burch was still alive, and Kate knew just where to get them.

In her own defense, if the patio door had been locked she would have gone back and told Matt her plan. But the door was open to let the sea breeze flow into the bungalow and the screen wasn't latched. She still hesitated before sliding it open. Someone inside was snoring. Probably Lenora, Kate thought vindictively. They were still here. Her original mission had been accomplished.

She went in anyway. Matt would scold her, but it would be worth it to see the look on his face when she told him what she had done. Besides, she was too caught up in the excitement of the moment to turn around now. He was wrong this time, that was all. They needed evidence and they needed it today, not next week.

Creeping softly across the plush carpet, Kate made her way through the clutter to the bar, its onyx top covered with glasses and overflowing ashtrays. After a few moments of rather distasteful searching, she smiled in triumph.

There it was, right where Chuck had left it. Using a napkin so as not to smudge his fingerprints, she picked up the sticky glass that had contained Chuck's sugary concoction. Kate smelled it and made a face. This was the one all right. Who else would have had a Scotch milkshake? Gingerly holding her prize, she turned around and started back toward the patio doors.

Before she had taken two steps her heart leaped into her throat and Kate froze in place. She could hear the sound of muted voices outside, growing louder by the second. Whoever it was, they were heading in her direction and coming fast.

"Oh, Lord," she moaned softly. "I'm going to get caught." Matt would be furious. Think, she told herself, just calm down, take a deep breath, and then get the heck out of there!

Lead-filled feet stumbled over each other as she slipped out of the room. She slid the screen door shut silently behind her and then practically fell into the flowering bushes lining the side of the patio, scrambling on her hands and knees for some kind of cover.

Adrenalin rushed through her trembling body. Her heart was pounding in her ears like an old-fashioned gong and Kate was sure anyone around her could hear it. With her mouth clamped shut she breathed deeply through her nose, trying not to make a sound.

Never again, she promised herself. Never again would she do something like this. She only hoped she could get out of there in one piece this time.

Kate leaned back against the cool stucco of the bungalow wall and tried to calm herself as her eyes adjusted to the gray morning light. The angry male and female voices were practically on top of her now, and she could clearly make out the shapes of two people approaching the patio as she peered through the leaves. They turned in her direction and Kate tried to shrink back still farther into the bushes.

It was Chuck and Lenora! Then who was asleep and snoring inside? A partygoer too drunk to make it home, no doubt. Her heart started hammering even louder in her chest. She could have been caught at any time.

"Did you hear something?"

"You're paranoid, Chuck," Lenora said derisively. "That was just the wind, or more of your overactive imagination."

Kate could hear the sound of the screen door sliding open, then one of them turned on a lamp inside and light spilled out onto the patio, bathing it in a soft glow.

"You had a hell of a nerve to come looking for me." Lenora's strident voice carried clearly across the quiet patio to Kate's hiding spot. She winced at the lash of the woman's tone. "Don't ever do it again." How could any man stand to live with someone like her?

"I don't care what you think, Lenora," Chuck shot back. "I'm leaving this morning. With or without you."

"You're overreacting again. Besides, I've already made plans for this week."

"And I'm sure they include your latest stud, the one who almost got killed last night."

"It's not any of your business what I do." There was a pause in the caustic debate, and Kate smelled cigarette smoke drifting in the air. "You'd do well to remember who controls the purse strings around here."

"Fine." Chuck's voice was bitter. "You stay here and I'll go to Grand Cayman alone."

"I forbid it."

"The plane is mine, and I'll go where I want to. You can't stop me. I don't like what happened last night or that big guy and his woman snooping around."

"They weren't snooping. I invited them." Her voice grew sultry and she added, "At least, I invited Matt. You're making a big deal out of a simple robbery attempt, that's all."

"It doesn't feel right. You can stick around here and see what happens, but I don't believe in coincidences."

Kate heard the sound of doors opening and closing loudly, then silence filled the air. Had they gone their separate ways? She started to get up but had to freeze in an awkward squatting position when they started speaking again.

"All right. You convinced me. I haven't been there in a while, and I could use the change of faces."

Chuck uttered a short, curt laugh. "Don't you mean the change of bodies?"

"Jealous, dear?" Lenora chuckled throatily. "The hunting might not be too bad this time of year at that. But we'll leave later today. I want to see Matt again."

"You . . ." Kate didn't catch his mumbled expletive. "I'm leaving in an hour, take it or leave it."

The sound of slamming doors assaulted her eardrums again, then all was quiet. Kate forced herself to stay put despite the cramps in her legs from her squatting position. The minutes passed like hours, but no other sounds came from the bungalow. She waited a few more moments just to be sure, then at last decided it was time to get away.

She cautiously stretched her cramped legs out to return the circulation to them. Crouching up on her knees she started to crawl out of the bushes backwards along the wall of the house, carefully holding on to the dirty glass in her hand.

Kate froze as a shadow fell across the dimly lit patio. Chuck stood looking out at the ocean, his eyes darting around the area. She didn't move a muscle, didn't even breathe.

"Chuck, come here and get this suitcase down. Now!"

Kate winced as he hurled expletives at Lenora and huffed back into the house. She didn't waste any time at all scurrying along to the end of the wall. Then she stood up, broke into a dead run, and kept running all the way back to her own bungalow, bursting through the door and slamming it behind her.

As she stood there panting for breath, somebody tapped her on the shoulder. She jumped, turned around, and came face to face with a furious and raging Matthew Gage.

"Where the hell have you been?"

Kate evaded his grasp and carefully set the glass down on the coffee table. Holding onto her sides she tried to catch her breath. If the stitch just below her rib cage was any indication, she really needed to get in better shape.

"I'm waiting, Kate!"

Kate flopped into a chair near the table. "I—I've been out," she puffed, still short of breath.

"Tell me something I don't know. What's this?" He reached for the glass.

"Don't touch that!" she yelled, knocking his hand away from her prize.

His eyes pinned her back in the seat. Large and furious, he towered over her, his hands gripping the arms of her chair, trapping her in front of him. "What is that?" he asked, not allowing her to break eye contact with him.

"Fingerprints."

"What?" he roared, pushing himself away from her and staring at her incredulously.

"Proof of who Chuck really is."

"You mean you went . . ." Matt started pacing back and forth from the bedroom to the living room of their suite, running his hands through his hair in outrage. "No. I don't believe it. You didn't?"

"I did." Kate was really quite pleased with herself now that she was back safely with Matt.

He stopped in front of her, furious. "You little fool, what if they'd caught you?"

"They almost—" Kate clamped her mouth shut, dismayed by what she had nearly revealed to him. She had already decided the less he knew about her adventure the better off she would be. "I'm here, aren't I?" she taunted.

The dawning light in his eyes worried her, as

did the look on his face; it reminded her of a raging thundercloud moving across the sky, ready to roar.

"Tell me the whole story, and don't leave anything out," he ordered, pulling a chair around to face hers.

Hesitantly at first, then with relish, Kate told him everything, with the calculated omission of her terror and the news of Chuck and Lenora's imminent departure. The fear she would never reveal, and the news she would save as a bargaining chip, knowing what he would probably say next.

He said it. "You're going back home today." He pulled her out of the chair and into the bedroom. "Pack."

With great difficulty Matt controlled his instinct to shake some sense into her. How could she have put herself into such a dangerous situation? He'd known all along that she was too impulsive for her own good, and she'd just proven it to him for the last time.

Moving away from her he watched as she docilely opened her suitcase and began to arrange things in her bag. Matt frowned. Something was wrong. She had never taken his orders before without a full-blown fight. What was she up to?

"There's something else," he said warily. She just hummed and kept packing. "They're going somewhere, aren't they?" Kate hummed some more. "If you don't tell me where those two are going, so help me—"

She flashed him a brilliant smile. "Wouldn't

you like to know?" Carefully folding her white sundress, she added it to the bag.

He stilled her hands, clasping them in his. "I could get it out of you," he threatened.

"Mmm," she murmured, rubbing against him. "That sounds interesting. I think I might like that."

"Kathryn!"

A mischievous pout formed on her inviting lips. "Not in the mood?" she queried softly.

"I'm in the mood to shake you till your teeth rattle," Matt warned, but even he knew it was a bluff. That was part of the problem. It was impossible to stay very mad at her when she rubbed against him like this.

"That sounds interesting too." She winked at him.

Shaking his head in disbelief, Matt wondered what he was going to do with her. She would just follow him no matter where he sent her. If she went with him he might at least be able to curb her impulsive instincts.

He pulled her down to sit beside him on the bed. "Okay," he said with a sigh. "Let's hear it again, and this time I want it all."

"I'm going with you?" At his nod she filled him in on the important details her previous story lacked. "There. That's all of it. Aren't you proud of me?"

Matt just barely managed not to smile. He was proud of her in a way. One simply had to respect a woman with her gall and single-mindedness. "Make the reservations."

"For two?" she asked suspiciously.

"For two," he confirmed. "I knew you were too smart for your own good. This time I intend to keep my eyes wide open and on you every moment."

Kate smiled up at him. "I hope it's more than your eyes," she murmured, leaning seductively against him, her fingers kneading his shoulders.

Matt fell back onto the bed, drawing her on top of him, her mouth eagerly finding his. She ran her fingers through his thick hair down the sides of his neck to his buttoned shirt. With surprising speed she undid his shirt, her hands roaming over his bared chest with unconcealed desire.

"Still feeling a bit of an adrenalin rush are we, dear?" he teased.

"Is that a complaint?"

Matt grinned. "Just an observation."

He was tempted to give in and let her have her way with him, but something held him back. He had just about gone out of his mind with worry when he awoke to find her missing, and the problem wasn't over yet. The sooner they finished this case, the sooner Kate would be out of danger and he could relax. They didn't have the time to indulge themselves right now.

"I have an observation of my own to make," Kate whispered throatily. "Care to hear it?"

"I'd love to. But later, Kate." With deep regret he stilled her touch. "Make the reservations."

"What?"

His hand landed firmly on her backside before

he pushed her to a standing position. "We don't have time for this right now."

She stared at him in disbelief. He was serious! He was already packing his bag, not looking at her. "What are you doing?"

"Packing. Bob Hale's oceanographic foundation is in the Cayman Islands too, remember? Maybe that's where they're headed. Maybe it's some kind of base of operations. One way or another they're our only real clue so far and I don't intend to lose them."

Kate silently fumed as she finished gathering up her things. Fine. If he could turn his emotions off and on at the flick of a knob let him. "Later, Kate," she muttered, zipping her toiletry bag shut with a vicious pull. "We don't have the time, Kate."

"We don't. We've got to send that glass off to Fidelity to be analyzed for fingerprints, then book a flight to Grand Cayman."

She sighed. "I know, but—"

Matt's strong arms gathered her close from behind and his bold lips nuzzled her neck. Kate struggled to release herself from his hold but he had her firmly in his grasp.

"Later," he promised.

"Maybe."

Matt twirled her around to face him. "Definitely!" He kissed her with such passion and desire that Kate forgot everything but her need for him. "Take the rest while you can get it, Kate.

When this is all over it might be weeks before I let go of you."

"You," she said, hugging him fiercely, "make the most delightful promises."

CHAPTER TWELVE

"What are they doing?"

"Acting very suspicious," Matt replied, handing Kate the binoculars he had been using to observe Lenora and the man calling himself Chuck. "See for yourself."

Kate adjusted the binoculars to her vision and scanned the powdery white sand in front of the cluster of airy pink buildings.

"What's suspicious about lying in the sun on Seven Mile Beach? That's one of the things people come to the Caymans for."

"Most people. Not those two," Matt pointed out. "I wonder what they're up to?"

"At the moment," Kate replied, "it looks as if they're taking a nap." She sighed and rolled over on the large towel beneath her, looking up at the clear blue sky. "This is boring."

He chuckled, admiring the way Kate's long, cocoa-butter-coated legs glistened in the sun. "Most investigating is, Kate."

Their arrival on Grand Cayman had been quick and efficient, the clean, new, yet distinctly Caribbean airport processing them through immigration with a minimum of fuss. Their baggage had been checked for contraband, their tickets examined to make sure they had already booked return passage and therefore weren't planning on being a drag on the community, and they were on their way.

The apartment-style lodgings they had checked into were right on the beach, practically next door to the similar establishment where Lenora and Chuck were staying. It afforded them a good spot to keep an eye on the unusual couple and yet was still far enough away that they wouldn't be easily spotted doing so.

Not that such secrecy seemed needed. Chuck and Lenora hadn't done anything but lie on the beach and splash in the ocean. Lenora occasionally stirred herself and tried to pick up one of the bronzed young men wandering by, but she didn't seem too serious about it. Kate decided she was just doing it to keep her hand in and to irritate Chuck.

"Well," Kate said, "so far Chuck has consumed a triple-dip ice cream cone and six candy bars. He's making me sick just watching him. And I can't take much more of this sun in any case."

"Neither can I," Matt agreed.

"Maybe that's their plan. Wait for us to turn into sunburned heaps and then make their move."

"They don't even know we're here," he reminded her. "And we don't know what's going on or if they have a move to make. For whatever reason, Chuck just got jumpy and decided to throw us off by coming here. You're right about one thing, though," he added. "Their present activity seems calculated to bore anyone watching them to tears."

Kate stood up and picked up her towel. "I've had it. Stay out here and fry if you want."

"No." Matt stood up, collected the rest of their gear, and fell in step beside her as she headed back to their room. "I think they'll be staying put for quite some time. Meanwhile, let's go see what we can find out about Bob Hale's oceanographic foundation."

Kate sighed as they stepped inside out of the sun. "I thought we'd never get around to that."

"Are you questioning my methods?" he asked, pulling her slick body against his own. "Going to the foundation is the real reason we're here. Seeing what that pair is up to is just a sideshow."

She grinned and kissed him. "You've got that right. I'll just grab a quick shower and we can be on our way."

"Mmm." Matt managed to keep hold of her despite her coating of suntan oil. "I need a shower too. Last one in has to wait for the soap," he teased, racing her to the bathroom.

Quite a bit later, the squeaky-clean couple managed to catch one of the capriciously scheduled flights to Cayman Brac island. An equally capricious but blessedly short cab ride brought them within strolling distance of the rather unimpressive, dockside building housing the Robert Hale Foundation.

It looked more like a place where one could charter a day of deep-sea fishing or scuba diving than an oceanographic research facility. A small boat rolled gently in its slip near the front of the place, and rows of air tanks lined the weather-beaten wood facade. Inside they found a woman fitting the description of Hale's mistress Matt had obtained from Hale's diving buddies in Florida.

Her name was Polly, and she was a blond bombshell. It made Kate think again of how ludicrous it had seemed to even consider her a suspect in a murder-for-hire scheme. Polly could make her way in the world without risking having Bob Hale killed to do it.

More likely by far was the scheme she felt certain the analysis of Chuck's fingerprints would soon prove: the men had faked their own deaths for the insurance money. Chuck was actually Chad, and hanging around somewhere would be a man with a different face and name who was actually Bob Hale.

Kate could scarcely ask the young woman if there was a man vaguely resembling Bob Hale sharing her life and her bed, however, so she just kept her eyes and ears open and let Matt take the lead.

He did so with cunning if rather boorish aplomb. "Hi, there, little lady! Bob Hale around?"

Polly looked up from some kind of bookkeeping log and studied the couple intently. "Excuse me?"

"Bob Hale," Matt repeated jovially. "Bob and I go way back. Used to dive together in Florida, but then we kind of lost touch. Imagine my surprise when I come down here on vacation with my wife and see old Bob's name on the front of this place." He grinned broadly. "What's he got going here, some kind of charter service?"

"We're a research foundation," Polly replied. "And I'm afraid—"

Matt interrupted her with a whistle. "Foundation? Pretty fancy. What all do you do here?"

"Research." She frowned. "Mostly concerning the way the numerous shipwrecks in this locale have changed the habitats of various species of marine life," Polly explained, sounding as if reciting a well-rehearsed speech.

"Golly," Kate said, feeling the need to say something.

Matt glanced at her, laughter in his eyes. "You said it, darlin'."

"But I'm afraid I have some bad news for you," Polly interjected, looking at Matt seriously. "Bob—I mean Robert Hale—is dead."

Kate frowned when Polly turned her face away after delivering the news. She looked genuinely distressed. But that would be part of the act, wouldn't it? If Matt really had been an acquaintance of Hale's, he might know about his relationship with Polly, and she would be expected to act bereaved. But if she was acting, she was very good at it.

"Dead?" Matt asked.

Polly nodded. "He had a diving accident in Florida a little over a year ago," she explained. But again it seemed as if she were reciting a speech. "This foundation bears his name because he set it up and endowed it with the proceeds from his life insurance policy."

Kate's frown deepened. Polly's initial reaction when she'd mentioned Hale's death had been real, she was certain. The explanation of his accident, however, had the ring of a lie. Polly wasn't such a good actress after all. But what did this true grief with the expected false story mean?

Evidently Matt had noticed something too. "I'm very sorry to hear that," he said slowly.

"Yes, it was a shock." Polly seemed to be recovering her composure. With it came a hint of suspicion. "But we continue to carry on his work. It keeps us very busy," she said pointedly. "I'm sorry, I didn't catch your names."

Matt had been frowning thoughtfully. His expression cleared and he replied, "Gage. Matthew and Kate Gage."

Every time he called her his wife or tagged his name onto hers in that manner, Kate's heart skipped a beat. She tried to ignore it. "Shipwrecks, you said?" she asked.

"And their effect on marine life," Polly added quickly. "And as I said, it keeps us busy, so—"

"Having any luck?" Matt interrupted.

"Some." The muscles in her jaw suddenly clenched. "It's difficult to hold onto the real finds," she told him. It was hard to tell if she was angry at them for delaying her or at something else. "Scientific competition is fierce."

"Really murder, I'll bet," Matt said innocently.

Polly stood up. "I'm sorry, Mr. and Mrs. Gage, but I have a great deal of work to do. My condolences on the loss of your friend," she said to Matt. "Now if you don't mind . . ."

"Of course."

As she led them to the front door, they could practically feel her suspicion and hostility. Before she could usher them out, however, a deeply tanned man came through the door and Polly's entire demeanor changed. She smiled, her eyes took on a certain sparkle, and it was suddenly as if Matt and Kate had ceased to exist.

"Hi, Polly," the bronzed, shirtless man said. His eyes sparkled too. "Did you miss me?"

"Don't I always?" she replied happily. Then she remembered what she had been doing and turned back to Matt and Kate. "This is one of our researchers back from a dive. We have business to discuss. I'm sure you understand." She firmly steered them out the front door into the bright sunlight of the dock and shut the door behind them. They heard the lock click loudly.

"What the—" Kate started to mumble.

"Shh!" Matt held a hand up and crossed casually to the only window at the front of the building. He peered inside, his eyebrows arching. "Come here," he said quietly, motioning to Kate.

Kate stood on her tiptoes to look through the window, and saw the couple locked in a lover's embrace. Her eyebrows arched too, then she turned and pulled Matt away from the window.

"Darn. It was just starting to get interesting," Matt complained.

"Surveillance is one thing, but I refuse to be a Peeping Tom." When they were away from the building, she looked at him, glad to see he was just as befuddled as she was. "I don't know what the heck is going on here, but even a consummate plastic surgeon couldn't have made that guy out of Bob Hale."

Matt shook his head. "Not unless they sawed a section out somewhere. Bob Hale was a six-footer if I remember correctly from the file. Polly's paramour back there was about five feet six at the most."

"Did you catch her distress when she told us Bob was dead?" Kate asked. "New lover aside, that was real grief, Matt."

"Either that or she should be in Hollywood," he agreed. "And yet the rest of it she said almost by rote. The foundation's business, the way Hale died, that part any second-rate starlet could have read with more conviction."

Kate nodded and sighed. "What does it mean?"

"I don't know. Maybe we've got it right and Hale was alive but his dangerous sports finally caught up with him down here. Maybe we're imagining the whole thing and he really did die in Florida, and Polly's just feeling guilty for taking up a new lover so soon. Or maybe she did have him killed and what we thought was grief was just nerves."

"Do you really believe that?"

He shrugged. "Who knows? If the fingerprints from that glass prove that Chad Burch is alive, we can try Polly again. Otherwise we'll just have to write the Hale Foundation off as a dead end," he told her, although the idea obviously didn't sit well with him.

They walked along, heading vaguely in the direction of the nearby airport and using the time to mull over the confusing details of their talk with Polly. Finally they saw a cab heading their way and Matt waved his hand.

Behind the wheel of the cab, the driver smiled. "I see you, Gage," Angelo said quietly. "In fact, I can't miss you. Not this time."

The cab sped up. It bounced along, its front grill lined up with the couple walking at the side of the road. At first Matt thought the driver was simply anxious for the fare. Then he realized the driver had no intention of stopping at all. Kate and he were about to become human pancakes.

"Matt!"

"And us between a rock and a hard place. Run!"

The man had picked his spot well. On one side the shoulder dropped off sharply to the sea, too far down to jump. The other side of the road was lined by a high, rock-strewn embankment.

Matt grabbed Kate's hand and pulled her along as he attempted to climb the embankment, but kept slipping on the loose, sandy soil beneath his feet. The cab loomed closer. Finally Matt managed to get some small purchase on the rocky slope and tugged Kate up to him, just as the cab bounced off the bank inches from where they stood. It roared down the road, ground to a stop, then turned around for another try.

"Shoot him!" Kate screamed as they slipped back down into the path of the oncoming vehicle.

"With what? A spit wad?"

But it gave him an idea. He picked up a rock from the side of the road and hurled it at the cab's windshield. It missed, but the driver swerved involuntarily, again sweeping by them with mere inches to spare.

"I know that guy," Matt muttered as he picked up another rock. "He was one of the men in that Jaguar in Phoenix. Maybe he was even the one who tried to push us off the road with the semi."

Kate hugged him close, her knees threatening to give out on her. She looked down the road, seeing the cab turning around again. This time when she opened her mouth to scream nothing came out.

"Come on," Matt said.

He pulled her across the road to the steep drop-off, taking his stand near the precarious edge. If the driver made the slightest error when he tried to bump them over the side, he'd go over himself. Matt was going to make sure he made that error. He felt the weight of the rock in his hand and watched the cab careening down the road toward them once again.

When the speeding vehicle seemed almost on

top of them, he threw the rock as hard as he could. This time the missile found its mark. The windshield shattered, a weblike star of cracks appearing on the driver's side. Matt didn't wait to see what would happen. He grabbed Kate around the waist and practically threw himself and her out of the path of the cab and into the center of the road.

Angelo couldn't see. He threw his arm over his eyes in an instinctive reaction to the flying glass and stomped on the brake, forgetting about his targets in favor of saving himself. But it was too late. The cab slid to a stop half over the edge of the road, teeter-tottered for a moment, then dropped headlong toward the sea below.

Kate opened her eyes. She was on top of Matt in the middle of the road and the breath had been knocked out of her. "You could have warned me!" she gasped.

"What are you complaining about? I'm the one on the bottom." He rolled her off of him and got up slowly, then pulled her up as well. She was pale with shock, but seemed unhurt. "Let's get out of here."

"Is he . . ." She paused, afraid to go see what had happened to the cab.

Matt walked to the edge and looked down. "No. He's splashing around. I guess even bad guys wear seat belts."

"Shouldn't we go question him?"

"It would take too long," Matt replied, taking her hand and leading her away. She had to trot to keep up. "One of his friends might be hanging around. Or the local cops might show up, and I don't particularly want to get involved with any explanations right now. They might decide to kick us out of the country and we'd lose our only leads."

"Chuck and Lenora?"

"Right. They're all we have to go on right now, so we'd better get back and keep an eye on them."

"You know," Kate remarked as they hurried toward the airport, "all of a sudden, sitting in the sun on the beach watching those two sleep doesn't sound so boring after all."

CHAPTER THIRTEEN

It was heaven. Warm blue water to wash away her fear, and hot sun to bake away a stiff leg muscle she'd gotten when they'd dived out of the way of the cab. Yesterday seemed an eternity away, and Kate felt like a new woman. As she reclined on a towel watching Lenora and Chuck, she decided that they were even more boring today, but it didn't seem to matter. All that mattered was that Matt was there beside her and they were both alive.

Of course, there had been the disappointing news from the lab that morning. The fingerprints on the glass had been smudged too badly to make an identification, at least right away. There were other tests, some kind of laser technology to detect latent prints, but that would take time. And if they had to wait, she couldn't think of a better spot to wait in than the Caribbean, nor a better man to wait with than Matt.

"Another boring afternoon before us. I think I'll take a nap," Kate announced, pretending to stifle a yawn. "Get a head start on all that rest you said I'll be needing when this is over." She walked inside, casting a sly glance over her shoulder as she disappeared through the door.

Matt followed her into the bedroom, his eyes never leaving her gently swaying hips. "Sounds good to me." He casually began stripping off his clothes.

"I'm quite serious," she informed him.

"So am I."

He yanked back the light covering of sheets and spread himself out comfortably on the bed, taking up a large part of it. Kate ignored him, feigning indifference as she removed her chunky white necklace and matching bracelet.

"Are you avoiding me?" he murmured, reaching out as she passed by the bed and pulling her down beside him.

"No, just getting ready for my nap." She tried to roll away but he held her firmly in his grasp. "Time is of the essence, you know. We can't afford to waste it." Kate didn't dare look at him. He deserved a good teasing and her desire for him was written all over her face.

"You don't really want to sleep, do you?" His hands lightly skimmed over her legs, following the contours.

"I don't know." A pout formed on her lips, an appealing little-girl look with an all-woman goal, laughter clearly brimming in her blue eyes. "I'm trying to decide."

"Let me help."

"Which side are you on?" she asked, willingly lifting her hips as he removed her pants.

"Ours," he whispered, flinging away the last of

her light clothing. "You'll sleep much better later." His voice promised her everything.

Kate was trying to hold back, to make him use all his powers to seduce her into his way of thinking, but she wanted him too much. "I've decided," she said suddenly, rolling on top of him and pinning him to the bed.

Matt wrapped his arms around her, not about to let her change her mind. "That was fast."

"Oh, I knew all along," she whispered huskily as her mouth covered his.

His hands cradled her hips as their kisses became deeper, her mouth opening freely, giving and receiving with equal desire. Her eager touch inflamed him with a blazing hunger, each taste of her lips making him want still more. Kate aroused him to a fever pitch, her desperate longing for him careening them both toward the never-ending inferno of their need for one another.

Her breasts seemed to swell beneath his touch, their erect, rosy pink tips straining against his palms as he gently massaged her soft, yearning flesh. With his tongue he drove the slow-burning embers of desire past the point of games, until Kate's passion joined his own and burst into brightly leaping flames. As always he made her pay deliciously for her teasing, and she spurred him on with her fluttering touch and throaty whispers.

She felt as if his tongue left a trail of fire when he tasted his way along her body, her back arching in reaction to his touch on her softly rounded stomach. He drifted on, teasing her thighs briefly before returning to the very center of her womanhood, and Kate cried out at the shattering, intense pleasure that spread through her like wildfire. She was already out of control, but managed to use the last ounce of her willpower to pull him to her in silent demand.

Joined, they rode along the very tip of the flames, bursting through the blazing colors of the sun to find an elusive moment of matching fulfillment, then plummeted back in shuddering ecstasy, cooling one another with soft moans and kisses. Slowly, lightly, like a feather among the waves of heat around them, they floated gently into a relaxed sleep in each others' arms.

Of all the amenities provided by the management of their resort lodgings, Kate and Matt agreed that the native Caymanian cook who came in to fix their dinner every evening was by far the most charming. They had a lively discussion while he cooked, and Kate even got an opportunity to pick up some of the local patois.

He prepared fish that had been caught scant hours earlier, accompanied by all the equally fresh trimmings. The best part of the meal, however, was the delicious conch chowder, a staple of the Caymanian diet and the very soul of the Caribbean when prepared by a professional. The cook was every bit the pro, and discreetly disappeared as soon as his work was completed.

"What'll we do tonight?" Kate asked, moving

over to make room for Matt on the couch as they relaxed after the filling meal.

Matt slipped his arm around her shoulders, hugging her close. "First you are going to promise me you won't get mad."

She sighed dreamily. "How could I possibly get mad on a soft night like this?"

"That's the way to look at it. You can have a nice relaxing evening here in our suite."

Kate's dreamy smile vanished. She pulled away and looked at him suspiciously. "And what will you be doing?"

"The cook was telling me about some of the local, lesser-known hotspots. If Bob Hale was down here, that's the kind of place he would have frequented. I'm going to hit a few of them tonight, see if I can scare up somebody who might have known him—or someone like him."

She leaned back against him. "I'll come with you."

"No."

"But—"

"No, Kate. These aren't tourist nightclubs, they're rough island bars. I want your promise" he took her firmly by the shoulders—"that you won't follow me. It could be dangerous." No answer was forthcoming. "Promise me!"

Kate knew by the tone of his voice that he wasn't going to give in this time. Still, she scowled at him for a while. Truthfully, she'd had more than enough excitement for a few days, but it wouldn't do to make it too easy for him.

"Oh, all right," she said at last. "I promise I won't follow you."

He enveloped her in his embrace, hugging her close. "Thank you. If it's any consolation, barhopping isn't my idea of fun." He kissed her soundly. "I'd much, much rather be here with you, but we have to see if Bob Hale was ever here at all, and this seems like the best way to do it."

"You be careful," Kate whispered, "I'd hate to have to come looking for you."

"Kate," he warned.

"Just kidding. When are you going?"

"No time like the present."

He stood up and went into the bedroom, returning casually dressed in blue jeans and a black cotton shirt. He looked like one of the many tanned men who went to the Caymans for the excellent scuba diving, only a bit tougher, his shirt hugging his deep chest and emphasizing his heavily muscled arms. He kissed her again, then walked swiftly to the door.

"Lock and bolt this behind me," he ordered, his hand on the doorknob. "And don't you dare leave this room, either."

"Whatever you say, Captain," she returned, giving him a smart salute as he walked out the door. When he was gone, though, she stuck out her tongue in a gesture of defiance. "But I might just take a moonlight swim whether you like it or not."

Restless, she wandered around the suite, unable to pick up a book or relax now that she was alone. She cleaned up the rooms a little, trying to recapture the pleasant domestic mood she had felt earlier during dinner. It didn't work. Soon her thoughts drifted back over her recent adventures.

The thing that bothered her most was the uneasy feeling she had ruined the best evidence they had found to date. Her panicked crawl through the bushes outside Lenora's Acapulco bungalow had undoubtedly smeared the fingerprints on Chuck's glass. All that work for nothing.

As she paced back and forth in front of the window looking out at the moonlit beach, Kate's eyes strayed to the buildings where Chuck and Lenora were staying. So near and yet so far.

Then she grinned slyly. Why not?

Earlier they had seen the battling couple split up, Chuck heading for the hotel bar and Lenora to the pool in the central courtyard. It was obviously Chuck's intention to drown his sorrows, and Lenora, ensconced near a group of athletic young men, wasn't going anywhere either.

The more she thought about it the easier it seemed. She could just slip over to their bungalow, and since open doors seemed to be Chuck and Lenora's habit, pick up a glass or two. Any that didn't have Lenora's bright shade of lipstick would surely have Chuck's fingerprints on it.

Kate picked up the binoculars and peered across the beach, her grin growing even broader when she saw that there seemed to be some kind of party going on nearby. This was predestined. She would be able to blend in, grab a few glasses, and leave with no one the wiser. If she got into any trouble, plenty of people would hear a scream for help.

Matt would fly into another of his rages when he found out. But he would forgive her, especially if this time the fingerprints were usable and it brought the case to a swift conclusion. It's what they both wanted; to be out of danger with no other mysteries to solve but the one of how their lives would fit together from now on.

This time she even left a scribbled note for him, just in case he came back sooner than she expected. Thus rationalizing away all but the slightest trace of guilt, Kate left the room, her heart racing and filled with confidence. Lots of people were still strolling around the beachside resorts and she blended in with them, the tropical evening air warm and refreshing.

The bungalow was not really all that different from the one in Acapulco. No lights glowed within, nor was there any sound or movement. Boldly, Kate walked up to the patio door and knocked, listening intently for any sound. If someone came to the door she would run like crazy.

But the place remained as quiet as an empty church. With a deep breath she tried the door. It slid open easily. She slipped inside and stood perfectly still, waiting for her eyes to adjust to the dim light of the moon streaming through the open glass doors.

Finally she was able to see the outline of the furniture around the room. Taking the plastic bag she had brought with her out of her pocket, she tiptoed around collecting glasses, taking every one she could find. She could sort them out at her leisure later. Moving carefully so the glasses in the now-full bag wouldn't clink together, she retreated toward the pool of light near the open door.

"Moonlighting as a maid?"

Kate stopped in her tracks, staring at the dark shape standing in the doorway. The cold, masculine voice made the hair on the back of her neck stand up. Though she couldn't see his face, she knew it was Chuck. And he knew she wasn't the maid; her face was clearly defined by the light of the moon.

"N-no," she replied. She forced her panic-stricken mind to function, trying to come up with some excuse for being there. Scraping up all the elan she could muster and hiding the bag of purloined glasses behind her back, she told him in a bewildered tone, "You remember me, don't you? Kate Gage? We met in Acapulco? Well, I couldn't find my husband anywhere, and I remembered how taken Lenora was with him. When I saw her on the beach earlier today I thought—"

"Shut up, Katie dear," Lenora said as her shape joined Chuck's in the doorway. She flipped a switch and suddenly the room was bathed in light. The wicked-looking gun in her hand was pointed directly at Kate. "If that's really your name."

"I don't know what you're talking about!" It was hard to look incensed when she was about to faint dead away, but Kate did her best. "My name is Kate Gage. I'm on an island-hopping vacation with my husband, Matt. I know I'm probably just being a jealous wife, but the way Matt looked at you in Acapulco . . . When he disappeared this evening I thought that perhaps he and you might have gotten together." She bowed her head as if embarrassed. "I see I've made a silly mistake."

"You made a mistake all right," Chuck said derisively. "What's that behind your back? A souvenir of your visit to Grand Cayman, I suppose?"

Kate lifted her chin defiantly, anger burning in her eyes. "All right. So you caught me. It doesn't make any difference." She held up the bag of glasses. "We were going to get your fingerprints off of these, but it was only a formality," she lied. "Matt and I know all about your little scheme. You're through, Mr. Burch."

He looked at Lenora. "I told you. She knows."

"She does now, you idiot," his wife said with disgust. "But it doesn't matter. If they really had anything to go on she wouldn't be here, especially not alone." Lenora closed the door, pulled the curtains shut and stepped closer to Kate, the small but lethal pistol aimed at her stomach.

"Shoot her."

"Shut up, Chad. Your stupid friends will take care of her. For the money we're paying them they'd better," she said bitterly. She turned her attention back to Kate. "I'm right, aren't I? You're just following us and nosing around. And judging by Matt's performance in Acapulco and your pathetic one just now, I'd say he's a pro and you're just along for the ride." Lenora laughed. "Why, I'll bet he doesn't even know you're here, does he?"

Why deny it? Lenora had so much practice at telling lies she could obviously spot one instantly. Kate hefted the heavy bag in her hand like a weapon and opened her mouth to scream.

"Don't." The other woman leveled the gun right between Kate's eyes. "I'll use this if I have to. Drop the bag."

Kate's bravado crumpled and she did as she was told. There was a tinkle of breaking glass as the bag hit the floor. "You're right. We don't know anything yet. So why don't you just let me go? If you do anything to me—"

"I'm not going to do anything," Lenora interrupted calmly. She backed up to where her husband was standing and gave him the gun. "Chad here is going to take you to see his friends."

Chad took the weapon and pointed it at Kate but looked incredulously at Lenora. "What?"

"They should have stopped these two before now. This is Carson's problem, and you're going to dump it in his lap right where it belongs."

"But—"

"I know it's difficult for you, Chad, but try to be a man for a change."

"Matt isn't far away. He'll be back soon and come looking for me," Kate said desperately. "You'll never get away with this."

"He will if he hurries," Lenora said, then turned to her husband. "Get a move on, Chad.

Carson might not like you bringing someone to his island hideaway, but his displeasure will be far better than what Matt will do to you if he catches you kidnapping his little Katie."

"And what are you going to be doing? Chasing any male within ten miles as usual, I suppose?" Chad asked bitterly.

"Why shouldn't I? My husband's dead, remember? You're just my lover, and a poor one at that."

"Why you—"

"Shut up. The money is in my name, dear, and don't you forget it," Lenora told him curtly. "If I were you I'd save all your bravery for Carson. You'll need it. Now, if you'll excuse me, I think I'll turn in. I have an early tennis date." With that she sauntered past Kate and into the bedroom.

The woman's callousness made Kate sick to her stomach. She could see hatred in her husband's eyes too. "Don't listen to her, Chad," she said quietly. "Turn yourself in."

"Shut up and start walking," he ordered, waving the gun wildly. "She's right. Carson will know what to do with you, and he'll get the big guy you're with off our backs as well."

Slipping the little pistol into his pocket, he marched her outside and around the cluster of buildings to his car. Kate could hear voices beyond the thick foliage surrounding the parking area. Before she could open her mouth, though, Chad jabbed her in the back with the gun.

"Don't even think about it," he whispered. "Get in the car. You drive."

"This Carson person hasn't stopped Matt yet," Kate said as they pulled away from the resort. "What makes you think he can do it now? Face it, Chad, you're finished."

"You're the one who's finished." He gnawed at his lower lip and added in a worried mutter, "I just hope he doesn't feed me to the sharks right along with you."

When Matt returned around midnight to find Kate missing, he was perturbed to say the least. And anger was hardly the word for the feelings he had as he read the note she'd left him. Fury was a better word. He couldn't believe it. Then he decided he could easily believe it. Going to get another glass was just like her, foolish and impetuous.

Kate had gone and done something stupid. Again.

"Damn," he muttered under his breath as he made his way across the beach to the adjacent hotel. "I should have tied her up and left her in Phoenix."

He pounded on Chuck and Lenora's front door. Lenora answered, wearing little more than a wicked smile. The filmy negligee floated around her in the gentle breeze as she stood in the doorway, its gossamer fabric clinging in all the right places. Matt blinked, momentarily taken by surprise.

"Hi, big fella. Did you come all the way to the Cayman Islands looking for me?"

"Where's Kate?" he demanded, regaining both his composure and his worried frown.

Lenora licked her lips seductively. "Lost your little playmate, have you?" she asked. "Won't I do?"

"Listen, lady," Matt told her, "in the first place I wouldn't touch a bedhopper like you." He pushed on the door. It swung open with a bang and he strode into the living room, Lenora backing up before him, the first signs of alarm on her face. "In the second place I asked you a question, and you'd better answer it before I wring your conniving little neck. Understand?"

"I . . ." Lenora's voice trailed off, her back literally against the wall. She nodded.

Matt glared at her. "Now, let's try this again," he said in a quiet, threatening tone. "Where is Kate?"

Lenora shook her head. "I don't know."

"Ever seen a women's prison, Lenora?"

"What?"

"That's where you're going," he promised. All he had were theories, but the time for methodical checking was over. He had to know what was going on and he had to know right now. "But for how long, I wonder?"

Lenora looked at him defiantly. "I don't have any idea what you're talking about. And what's more," she added, "I don't think you do either."

"Don't underestimate me, Lenora," Matt replied with a caustic smile. "I can see to it you're charged with more than accessory to insurance fraud. How does accessory to murder sound? That would keep you in prison for quite a while. Think about it, Lenora. Growing old and fat, maybe getting killed in a fight, no men around . . ."

Evidently he'd hit her weak spot. "Wait!" she cried, her face pale. "Wait just a minute. What's all this about murder? Chad's still alive. He got me involved in this stupid insurance scam and—"

"Thank you. I was wondering if that's what was going on," he interrupted. "Now tell me the rest." Her face a mask of hatred, Lenora swung at his eyes with her inch-long fingernails. He caught her hand and held it at her side. "Careful, puss. You don't want to hurt me. Tell me what I want to know and I'll put in a good word for you."

"You don't know anything!"

"I know enough. I know that if you've done anything to Kate I'll see you rot in a cell."

The woman actually smiled. "I didn't do anything to her. Chad's flying her out to see Carson right this minute. A cell will be heaven compared to what he'll do to her."

"Lady . . ." He clenched his fists in fury, barely holding himself in check. "I've never hit a woman in my life, Lenora, but if you don't talk, so help me—"

"Go ahead, you big ape! Push me around. I can't tell you where she is because I don't know!" Lenora yelled triumphantly.

Matt shook her by the arms. "What?"

"It's an island somewhere. Carson owns it. I've never been there, so I don't know where it is or how to get there."

"When will Chad be back?" he demanded.

Lenora shrugged. "He might not come back at all," she said carelessly. Matt's grip on her had gone slack, and she took the opportunity to slip away from him, going to a table near a plushly upholstered couch and lighting a cigarette. "He went to see Carson unannounced," she continued, exhaling a stream of smoke. "That isn't done. Like as not poor old Chad is in just as much hot water as little Katie."

"You really are a sweetheart," Matt said, looking at her with disgust. "It doesn't matter to you how much blood is on that money, does it?"

"Not a bit." She walked over to him, running her fingers up and down his shirt front. "There isn't anything you can do, you know. She's gone and so is Chad, and I don't have the slightest idea where to find them. Why don't you just give it up? You'll never beat Carson anyway."

Matt chuckled mirthlessly. "Are you willing to bet the rest of your life on that, Lenora?"

"You don't really want to put me in jail, do you, Matt?" she asked, pressing her hips against him.

The woman had no sense of decency and about as much loyalty as a rattlesnake. He forced himself to smile at her. "Maybe not," he replied softly. "Who is this Carson character anyway?"

"He's a dealer in death, both real and imaginary, with an army of men behind him. Need money? Carson's your man. For a share of your life insurance he can fake your death, give you a new face and a new identity." Lenora grinned. It was obvious she loathed the man, but was fascinated by him as well. "Then he's got you. He helps you invest your money in his other business interests—for a healthy share of the profits. Complain, step out of line, and he'll have one of his minions slit your throat."

"If he stays that close, you must have some way of contacting him."

She shook her head. "He does the contacting, and only then to bleed more money out of us." Lenora sneered. "He even makes me send money to my daughter, to keep up the illusion she has a loving mommy somewhere. It really burns me up."

"A waste of good cash," Matt said, swallowing his revulsion.

She looked at him, her eyelids lowered seductively. "If you *could* stop him, you and I could take all of the money, Matt. We could have a really good time. If you're really going to go after him, why not make it for something worthwhile?"

"But how would I stop him?" he asked, running a finger along her jaw. "I mean, it is very tempting, Lenora. But you said there's no way I can even find him. If I could"—he pulled her closer, letting her feel his strength—"I could stop him."

Her eyes narrowed. "And you said you

wouldn't touch me," she replied, sticking out her lower lip in a pout.

He shrugged. "What can I say? I was worried about Kate. But if I could have the money *and* you . . ."

"I knew we'd see eye to eye eventually," she said in a breathy whisper. "There might be a way. Carson is supposed to have a headquarters of sorts around here somewhere."

"On Grand Cayman?"

Lenora licked her lips. "All those muscles and brains too. That's right. If you could find the base, you could probably force someone to lead you to the island. Chuck said they keep a lot of explosives there. You could blow it up or something, and none of them would bother us again."

"Good idea. Thanks," Matt said curtly, pushing her away. She landed on the couch in a very unladylike posture. "I knew a sick mind like yours would have some kind of contingency plan."

"You . . . You . . ." Lenora sputtered in outrage.

"I'll visit you in prison, Lenora."

"You're a fool!"

"Yeah, I know. Ain't love grand?" Matt grinned. "Now if you'll excuse me, touching you has left me with the urgent need to go sterilize my hands."

CHAPTER FOURTEEN

Kate had no idea where she was or where Chad was taking her. All she knew was that they had been flying over water for quite some time. It would be dawn soon. The first rays of the sun had just begun to glimmer on the rippled surface of the ocean.

She had nursed a tiny hope when Lenora had mentioned an island hideaway. The trip would require a plane or boat, and therefore a chance to escape. If they had to fly, Chad couldn't keep a gun on her while going through airport security. If they went by sea he might have to leave her alone long enough to give her an opportunity to jump overboard.

When he'd forced her to drive to a small airport her hopes had soared. Then she had remembered that Chad Burch was a pilot. The field was secluded, nobody even approached them, and they were airborne in minutes, with Chad in control of a twin-engined private plane.

He didn't have a gun on her now, but she couldn't very well jump out and fly to safety. So she watched the ocean slip by beneath them and tried to keep her mind off her desperate situation by asking Chad questions.

"Why did you do it, Chad?"

"The name's Chuck now. Chuck Aspin. Get it? Before I was a Burch tree, now I'm an Aspin tree." He laughed without much humor. "I did it for the money. Why else?"

"But to leave your whole life behind?"

"Life? What life?" he asked derisively. "Let me tell you something about Chad Burch. He was a loser. He was a boring kid, went to a boring college, and ended up in a boring job." He sucked on his ever-present lollipop.

Kate felt her stomach lurch as he banked the little plane to the left. "But you quit the job, started to make changes. Surely prospecting was exciting?"

"Not when you don't have enough money to do it right, it's not," he replied. "When I wasn't sitting around listening to old geezers talk about some treasure trove they'd found and lost, I was tramping around the desert, slowly becoming just as loony as they were." He glanced briefly around the cockpit of the plane. "This baby's brand-new, fitted with all the latest gear. I paid for it in cash, and I can afford to keep it fueled. It takes money to find gold, Kate, and the only way I could get that money was to fake my own death and collect the insurance."

Kate's eyes widened. "You're still prospecting?"

"You bet. How else am I going to get away from that miserable harpy?"

"Lenora?"

He nodded, his expression one of disgust. "That's another thing about Chad Burch. He was dumb. Since money was the only thing his wife ever talked about, he thought getting some for her would be the way to make everything rosy again."

"It didn't, obviously."

"It turned her into a monster. I wouldn't even get enough money out of her to keep prospecting except that it keeps me out of her way while she chases other men."

"At least she sends money to Stacy."

Chad laughed bitterly. "Only because she has to. She made the mistake of trying to abandon Stacy, a move Carson thought might cause suspicion. It ticked him off, so along with a sort of monthly maintenance fee he charges to provide protection and such, he makes Lenora write checks for the house in Tucson and Stacy's education."

"Magnanimous of him," Kate remarked sarcastically.

"Lenora made him mad. He could snuff her out like that," Chad said, snapping his fingers, "or just take the money for himself as payment for her stupidity. But he knows how much it gauls her to send that cash to Stacy. I think he does it to torture Lenora, remind her who's in charge."

Kate looked at him curiously. "How about you? Do you begrudge giving Stacy money?"

"I had planned on giving her a share all along.

She's a good kid, smart too. I hadn't done right by her and I knew it. But Lenora got the money and . . ." Chad trailed off with a resigned shrug. "Maybe if I strike the mother lode I can still do something."

He had been talking openly, almost as if these were things he had wanted to get off his chest for a long time. It occurred to Kate that even though he was a criminal, unlike Lenora he still had some traces of humanity left in him. Perhaps she could use that to her advantage.

"Any regrets, Chad?" she asked.

"I would have done things differently, that's for sure," he replied. "Maybe I wouldn't have done it at all, I don't know. I had the brass ring and Lenora stole it. I'm not much better off than I was before. In some ways it's even worse. Too late now, though."

"No it's not, Chad," Kate told him. "You're involved in insurance fraud, and you'll have to pay for that. But you can still put things right. Help me. Turn this plane around and get me back to Matthew Gage."

He shook his head and laughed curtly. "You still don't understand, do you? Carson *owns* me—body, soul, and bank account. I have a new identity and all, but it's one of his making. Chad Burch is dead. It's no trouble to kill a dead man, Kate."

"Matt can help," she assured him.

"No he can't. No one can." He peered through the windshield and began nosing the plane toward what in the predawn gray looked like a dark smudge on the glistening sea below. "Better brace yourself. The runway's short and pretty bumpy."

"Please, Chad!"

Kate watched the smudge turn into a spot of land that grew larger and larger before her eyes. Even in big jets takeoffs and landings were not her favorite parts of flying. With just enough early daylight to see the runway, Chad made his final approach. She swallowed dryly and held onto the edges of her seat.

"No. Not a chance. My life may not be a whole lot better than before, but at least I'm still breathing."

The plane bounced and jumped as it hit the rough runway carved into the overgrown jungle of Carson's private island. When they rolled safely to a stop at last, men carrying some kind of guns slung over their shoulders appeared from out of the dense foliage nearby and approached the aircraft warily.

Kate made a final, desperate attempt. "Get word to Matt. Tell him where I am."

"It wouldn't do any good."

"Yes it would! He's going to stop Carson one way or another, Chad."

"Nobody can stop Carson," he said flatly.

"Matt can. He *will.* Help him, bring him here. Don't you realize what you're doing? Insurance fraud is one thing, but Carson is a murderer. By bringing me here you're helping him, Chad, and when Matt does break this ring he'll see to it you go to death row right along with the rest of these killers."

"Maybe Carson won't hurt you."

The armed men were getting closer. "Do you believe that?"

"No. I guess not."

"Then help me!"

Chad frowned, then the doors of the plane jerked open, cutting off whatever he was about to say. One of the men, evidently the leader, stuck the barrel of a machine gun in Chad's stomach. Another stood on the other side of the plane, staring stonily at Kate. He, too, pointed his gun into the aircraft.

"You were told never to come here again," the leader told Chad, emphasizing his point by jabbing him in the stomach.

"Hey! Relax, guys!" he said, putting his hands in the air. "I brought Carson a present."

If Kate had tried to envision the man behind this horrific scheme—and she had from the moment she'd been kidnapped—she couldn't have come up with a more likely candidate than the man who stood before her now.

He was about six feet tall, very thin, with a hawklike nose and a cap of slick, shiny black hair. The skin of his face and hands, darkly tanned and with a dry, leathery appearance, seemed stretched tight over his bones, giving him the look of a well-preserved yet very old man.

And those eyes. They were coal black, empty of any remotely human emotion; looking into them was like gazing into the depths of a dark, still pond. Kate shivered beneath his abysmal gaze as he paced slowly back and forth in front of a wide expanse of windows overlooking the sea far below.

Under the guns and watchful eyes of Carson's guards, she and Chad had been marched from the runway, along a rocky beach, past a scattering of small buildings, and up a long, winding series of steps. At the top of a craggy escarpment they were then taken into a much larger building, obviously Carson's home and command post.

There the uniformed guards had left them in the hands of three equally well-armed but more casually dressed men who took them for a sunrise audience with Carson. He had spoken briefly with one of the men, and had been pacing and staring at them ever since.

They were in a large, echoing chamber, which ran along the entire front of the circular house, with white marble tile underfoot and a sharply slanted ceiling far overhead. A balcony lined by a shiny brass railing arched above and behind them, with curving staircases giving access to this second story situated at each end of the big, semicircular room.

In front of them the windows stretched off to both sides and from floor to ceiling, like a big one-hundred-eighty-degree movie screen. Chrome, glass, and white-fabric furniture divided the space into sections according to use; a living room grouping to their left; bar and entertainment area to their right; and the officelike environment where they now stood.

Carson paced in front of a free-form desk that looked like a massive, highly polished piece of driftwood with a flat working surface carved into it. He would take three steps forward, turn, then take three steps back, his bony hands clasped behind him and his eyes never leaving their faces.

Suddenly he stopped pacing. His minions seemed to shrink back so as not to be included in his wrath. When he finally spoke, his voice was as crisp as dry leaves crackling on a chill autumn day.

"I am going to feed you to the sharks, Mr. Burch. One tiny piece at a time." Carson smiled at the thought, then paused to adjust the lapels of his white tropical-weight suit coat. He studied Chad closely. "But before I do, I want to know what could have possibly made you do this."

"This woman was following us and snooping around," Chad replied. His whole body seemed to tremble as he spoke. "She knows, Carson. And there's a guy with her, a private cop I think, and I—"

"And you thought I wasn't aware of their presence in either Acapulco or on Grand Cayman?" Carson interrupted. Chad nodded eagerly. "I see. In other words, you not only disobeyed my orders never to come here again, you are also calling me a fool."

Chad's mouth dropped open. "No!"

All three of the armed men around them shook their heads sadly, their expressions full of disbelief that anyone could be so stupid. Guns or not, Kate could see that their fear of Carson was absolute.

"I have known about Mrs. Asher and Mr. Gage for quite some time. The matter was well in hand. For you to think otherwise was a mistake. For you to come here to tell me about it was an even bigger mistake." Carson shook a thin finger at him as if scolding an errant child. "But your biggest mistake of all was bringing this woman with you. It is a mistake you will regret most profoundly. A fatal one, I am afraid."

"It was Lenora!" Chad cried. "She made me do it."

Carson actually laughed, a wheezing sound Kate found horrifying. "Yes, that I can believe. The beautiful Lenora would know what I would do to you, thereby ridding herself of you, and I imagine she harbored some hope that sending the woman here would put me in danger, thereby ridding herself of me as well." He shook his head in something akin to admiration. "If she had any loyalty at all I might hire her to work for me. As it is I think she will be following you into the bellies of the fish."

He waved a hand at his minions, one of whom grabbed Chad and started pulling him away. "Put him somewhere to think about his transgressions for awhile," Carson said. "I'll deal with him later."

Kate turned her head away as the man dragged Chad out of the room. If he was locked up somewhere he couldn't get word to Matt. She didn't know if what she had said to him had convinced him to help her in the first place, but at least it had been a ray of hope.

"Well." Carson strolled over to Kate and gazed at her. "I find my emotions curiously mixed about your presence here, Mrs. Asher. May I call you Kate?"

She looked at him. Though tired from lack of sleep and the seesawing of her emotions, hatred still burned in her eyes. "I don't care what you do. I just hope I live long enough to see Matt feed *you* to the sharks!"

"On the one hand, Kate," he continued, ignoring her hostility, "Gage will undoubtedly come looking for you, and since he has proven himself to be a very resourceful man, that could be troublesome." He gave her one of his emotionless smiles. "On the other hand, now that you are here, I suppose I could consider you bait. My men here are of a much different caliber from the ones he has encountered thus far. It will be an interesting test."

"Test?" Kate managed a vicious smile of her own. "Matt will take you apart piece by piece."

Carson shook his head. "No. He will most surely die, as will you. It is a pity in a way. He has been good for my forces, shown me the weak among my ranks. And you"—he reached out a hand to caress her cheek—"are very pleasant to look at."

"Don't touch me!" She recoiled from him in revulsion. "Get it over with. Kill me just like you killed my husband, you filthy murderer. But don't touch me again or I'll claw your eyes out."

One of Carson's henchmen started to grab her, his face showing shock at the way she had spoken to his boss. But Carson merely frowned and waved the man back.

"It was necessary to kill your husband. He was fairly good at his job, and got a bit too close to the truth. So did the other one, Tynly I believe his name was." He spoke as if explaining nothing more than a regrettable business necessity. "I have to protect my clients, you see. They pay me quite handsomely to arrange their false deaths, and afterward I supply them continued safety and financial guidance."

"You blackmail them. Once they cross the legal line you have them under your thumb. Then you use their money to fund other unholy schemes," Kate said hotly.

He shrugged. "I am a businessman."

"You're a killer!"

"I do what I have to do to survive in a cruel world," he said calmly. "I do not force these people to join my flock. I contact them, yes, people who are greedy and need money. I show them how they can get that money, then help them do so. My help does not come cheap, but they are eager to pay."

"You won't get away with it."

"But I have. I am!" he replied. "Do you think Fidelity is the only company I have stung? Look around you." He swept his hand to indicate his island. "I rule an empire from here. Through my network in America and Mexico people get new faces, new names, then step into the new identities I create for them." His gaze returned to her face. "And yes, I own them. They have their money, but I control them, and therefore all their millions."

Kate's eyes widened, her lip curled in disgust. "Why don't you just kill them?"

His harsh laugh echoed through the room again. "I could. Just as I could wait until the insurance companies settle and then take it from them. I am safe on my island, and they can hardly go to the police, after all."

"Then why don't you?"

"That would compromise my situation," he replied with an evil sneer. "This way the money is spread out, under my control yet not under my name. I stay here and pull their strings. Besides," Carson added slyly, "I enjoy my puppets. I like to watch them dance to my tune."

Kate backed away from him, even more sickened than before. He was smart, and powerful—and quite insane. Carson was a psychopath with absolutely no concern for people and their lives save what profit could be made from using them. He horrified her.

But most of all he brought from deep within her that dark, hidden side of herself. She wanted him dead. She wanted to make him pay for her anguish and that of Gloria Tynly, and for a little boy who would never see his father again.

"When Matt gets here he'll kill you, and I

want to be here when he does," she said, her voice harsh and unfamiliar in her ears.

Carson glared at her, his face a hideous mask of fury. "No, I shall kill him, and you shall watch." He cocked his head to one side as if a thought had just entered his evil brain. "Wait," he said, going to his desk and typing something into a computer keyboard.

"Yes, I thought so. I have even more plans for you, Kate Asher. I see that during your employment at Fidelity you were persuaded to take out a fair-sized life insurance policy. It would be a shame to waste the money on some relative." He chuckled with psychotic glee. "You shall become a member of my flock, dance to my will, stay here under my roof until I tire of you."

"Never!"

"You would rather die?"

"Yes!"

Carson's eyes narrowed for a moment, then his face went blank, the total lack of emotion even more frightening than his grotesque smiles and grins. He waved his hand in dismissal.

"Take her away. I'll keep her alive until Gage shows up, if he makes it this far. If he does, don't kill him unless you have to. It will amuse me to watch them say their last good-byes."

The cell was just that, a tiny cubical with the barest necessities, amid others just like it in some kind of dungeon deep beneath Carson's house. Kate had eaten three surprisingly decent meals so far, the first out of hunger, as it came late the day Chad had brought her to the island.

Exhausted, she had slept, then ate breakfast the next day mainly out of boredom, and lunch because she realized that even if she didn't have an appetite she had to keep up her strength.

Matt would come. She felt it deep inside, right next to the pain she felt knowing the danger he would face to get there. When he did arrive, when he found her, she didn't want to be a weakened burden he would have to carry to safety. She wanted to be what she had tried to be all along, a partner who could help him destroy the evil men upstairs.

When the guard brought dinner she waited until he had left and then wept, as quietly as possible, not wanting them to think they had broken her. What if Carson hadn't been boasting? What if Matt really didn't stand a chance against his troops? It was all her fault. If she had only listened to him, let him handle things his own, slow-but-sure way.

She wasn't used to hearing the guard's voice except at mealtimes, and jumped when he thumped on the door of her concrete and steel cell.

"Back away from the door."

"I haven't finished eating yet," she replied curtly.

"I said back away!" he shouted through the small, barred opening in the door.

Kate did as she was told, hearing the key in the heavy latch, watching the door swing slowly open. She prepared her stomach for the sickening sight of Carson coming to try to talk her into making a deal for her life insurance money again. What she saw when the door banged against the wall was even worse.

"Matt!"

She started toward him, but one of the guards on either side of him pointed a gun at her. She watched helplessly as they struggled with Matt's unconscious form, dumping him unceremoniously on the bed against the wall. The small cot creaked beneath his bulk.

"With Carson's compliments," one of the guards bit out savagely. "But not for long. Gage is going to pay for all the damage he did."

The door slammed shut, and Kate was alone with her savior. "Oh, Matt! What have they done to you?"

He was wearing black swimming trunks and a thin black cotton shirt. Wherever his skin was exposed she saw bruises and scratches. The skin around one eye was bruised, and a trickle of blood could be seen at the corner of his mouth. He moaned loudly when she lifted his head and sat down on the bed, cradling it in her lap.

"Speak to me!"

One eye opened a tiny slit. "Are they gone?"

Kate stared at him. "What?"

"Are they gone?" he whispered again.

Her befuddled mind finally grasped what he was asking. "The guards? Yes, they're gone. Are you all right?"

In way of answer he snaked one of his arms

around her neck and pulled her head down to his, kissing her soundly. "Bloody but unbowed," he replied when he finally released her. "Always remember: if you find yourself hopelessly outnumbered and nothing else will work, go down with the first punch that feels serious enough for them to believe they knocked you out."

"First punch!" she exclaimed, gingerly touching his face. "You look awful!"

"Thanks," he replied dryly. "The only thing they can take credit for is the black eye. I got the rest of the damage all by myself, scrambling through the surf and the jungle to get to the encampment." He ogled her rakishly, a bit incongruous considering the darkening bruise under his eye. "You, on the other hand, look good enough to eat."

"Will you be serious! The only reason they didn't kill you is that Carson has some kind of ceremony planned. He gets his kicks out of watching people beg, Matt," she told him, shivering uncontrollably. "He's a foul, evil—"

"I know." He sat up and put his arms around her, willing his strength to flow into her. "It wasn't in my plans to get caught, I assure you. He's practically got a small army out there."

Kate finally stopped shivering, feeling his warmth and power washing over her, pushing aside her fear. "Didn't you know what you would be walking into?" she asked. "Come to that, how on earth did you find me in the first place?"

"I got a little unwilling help from Lenora," he replied, grinning at the memory of tricking her.

"She told me about a base Carson has on Grand Cayman."

"Is that where we are? Still in the Caribbean?"

"I was hoping you knew."

"Nobody offered me any specifics," she returned, then looked at him skeptically. "What do you mean, you were hoping I knew? Don't you?"

"Not really. I stowed away on some kind of supply boat at Carson's Grand Cayman base late last night. We were at sea quite some time, but it still feels like the tropics. Other than that I don't know."

"Does anyone else know we're here?"

Matt shook his head. "I didn't have time to contact the authorities, if that's what you mean, and I'm not sure they would have listened to such a wild tale anyway."

"I suppose not," Kate agreed dejectedly. She hugged him again. "I'm just glad you found me."

"It wasn't easy. Lenora just pointed me in the right direction. I decided it was time to talk to the late Bob Hale's mistress, Polly, again, to see if she knew anything about this place."

"The *late* Bob Hale? Then he isn't living under an assumed name and face like Chad was?"

Matt shook his head. "No. He was for a while, using his money to continue diving in dangerous waters to explore old shipwrecks. His luck finally ran out. Polly finally started talking and told me that Carson arranged a diving accident when Hale actually found some sunken treasure."

"No wonder her grief was fresh," Kate said. "And it fits. Carson likes to have complete control over his flock, as he calls them. He wouldn't want Hale to have any money he might not be able to get his slimy hands on. Chad still prospects for gold, trying to get out from under Carson's thumb and away from Lenora." She sighed. "Or at least that was his plan. He disobeyed Carson by coming here and Carson is going to get rid of him too—if he hasn't already. It's too bad. I think I almost had him convinced to help me."

"Well, Polly was very helpful once I convinced her which side I was on. She took me to Carson's base and showed me how I might gain access, even knew about the supply boat, though she didn't know where they went." He thoughtfully rubbed the two-day growth of beard on his chin. "I get the feeling Carson's flock is a pretty restless group."

Kate laughed without much humor. "Can you blame them? He promises them riches, then once he fakes their deaths and has them under his control, he uses them to shield his own identity while investing their insurance money," she explained. "They're like slaves. It's their own fault, of course, but you can't help but feel a little sorry for them."

"Yes, Polly told me all about it. After Hale died she formulated a scheme for getting away from Carson too; she runs a pretty profitable charter service on the sly. But Carson found out and threatened to get rid of her as well." He grinned. "She and that guy we saw her with wanted to come with me and kill Carson with their own bare hands."

Kate's eyes smoldered with fury. "I know the feeling very well."

"Now you listen to me," Matt said, taking her by the arms and giving her a gentle shake. "We know most of the story now, and the only thing we're going to do is get away from here so we can tell somebody. We leave the retribution to somebody else. Got it?"

She swallowed her anger, feeling frustration burning through her. "If we can get away, and if anyone will believe us."

"We'll get away," he assured her, wishing he felt as confident as he sounded. Then his iron will clamped down on any doubt. He would save the woman he loved at any cost. "As for making someone believe us, I don't think it will be too hard to convince the members of Carson's flock to come forward to testify."

"Why should they?" she asked.

"Because the whole deal will start coming apart once we get out of here anyway," Matt explained. "By coming forward they might shave some time off their jail sentences. If Polly is any indication of how the rest feel, I imagine they'll view it as a relief to have this nightmare over with at last."

"I know Chad would—if he's still alive."

"If he is we'll take him with us. All the police would have to do is check his fingerprints to prove we're telling the truth about this scheme."

Kate nodded, but she was still frowning. "That still leaves my original question," she reminded him. "How are we going to get out of here, let alone take Chad with us?"

"Good old Chad," Matt mumbled. He started to smile, a plan forming in his mind. "This might not be impossible after all."

"What?"

"Nothing. Any ideas on where Chad might be?"

Kate shrugged. "Probably on this level with us. There are a lot of cells in this dungeon."

He was even starting to feel optimistic. "We'll check them all on the way out. If we find him, we're home free."

"And just how do you propose to get out?" she asked curiously.

Matt looked surprised. "What's the matter, Kate? Haven't you ever seen any old prison movies?"

CHAPTER FIFTEEN

"You've killed him!" Kate yelled, pounding on the cell door. "He's dead!"

She heard the clanking of keys and then the footsteps of a guard as he came tramping down the concrete corridor to her cell. She sat down on the bed next to Matt's sprawling form and put her face in her hands, wailing and crying as if her heart were broken.

"Are you crazy, lady?" the guard asked. "We just tapped him with the butt of a gun. I'm surprised a guy his size even felt it. Must've hit him just right."

"Just right? He's dead!"

The guard peered through the door. The big man did indeed look dead, lying on the cot on his stomach with his arms and legs askew as if he'd thrashed his last breath away.

"He's faking."

"No, he's not! He's dead!" Kate cried. "You killed him." Now to bait the hook. She looked up at the guard and told him spitefully, "Carson wanted him alive and you killed him. I'd hate to be in your shoes."

The guard was hooked. "He can't be dead!" he said nervously, putting the key in the door and unlocking it. "Not that he didn't deserve it. The bastard went through ten guys, broke every window at the front of the house, and threw Carson's desk into the sea. He's a gorilla. He can't be dead." In anguish, the man opened the door and stepped over to Matt's body. He bent over and put a finger on the pulse in Matt's throat. "Wait a minute . . ."

Matt raised straight off the bed, the back of his head colliding with the guard's jaw. Something popped, but it wasn't Matt's tough skull. The guard went down in a heap.

"That's for calling me a gorilla."

"Did you really throw Carson's desk out the window?" Kate asked as she handed him the guard's gun.

"Most of his furniture too. I didn't intend to, though. I was throwing the stuff at his goons and they ducked. It's their fault."

Kate chuckled quietly as they crept to the open cell door. "And the windows?"

"That wasn't my fault either. I was just sneaking along the front of the house looking for you when they came in the room and saw me. Carson told them not to kill me, so they shot over my head and . . ."

"Instant ventilation?"

Matt nodded. "Now, hush. I'll give the blow-by-blow some other time." He cautiously poked his head out the door and looked down the corridor, then pulled it back in fast. "Company coming," he told her, pushing her back to the bed. "Sit there and look sexy."

"What?"

"Lure him in, dear," Matt whispered, then took up a position behind the heavy steel door.

Although she felt anything but seductive at the moment, Kate did as she was told, sitting on the bed with her legs crossed and her skirt hiked up high on her thigh. Another guard appeared in the doorway, pistol drawn and at the ready.

"Hi, sport," Kate said, winking at him. "You're friend wasn't up to it. Care to try your luck?"

The man frowned and took a step into the room. Matt gave the door a quick, hard shove and the guard flew back out into the corridor, his unconscious form sliding down the opposite wall.

"Sport?" Matt asked sardonically.

Kate shrugged and stood up. "I watch old movies too, you know."

Matt grabbed the second guard's gun, and he and Kate continued down the narrow corridor. The first cell they came to was empty, as was the next. The third, however, held the jackpot.

"Hello, Chad," Kate whispered.

"Good Lord! How did you—"

"I told you Matt was good," she told him. She fumbled with the keys she had taken from the guard. Matt kept watch. "To tell you the truth, even I didn't know how good until just a few minutes ago," she added when she finally found the right key and Chad joined them in the hallway. "But if you listen to him," she said, pausing to look at Matt, "like I should have, maybe he can get us out of here."

Chad started to object, looked at the cold, hard glare Matt gave him, and changed his mind. "Might as well. I wouldn't be around much longer anyway, so what have I got to lose?"

"Do you know if there's anybody else down here, Chad?"

He shrugged. "Like who?"

"Carson's new recruits, maybe?"

"I doubt it. He doesn't keep them on the island anymore, like he did with me," Chad explained. "It's a new policy. I guess he got worried about them getting too friendly with each other and staging a mass revolt."

"They realize their mistake that soon?" Matt asked.

"You bet. Carson lets you in on the facts of life as soon as your false obituary hits the papers, but by then it's too late—he's got you where he wants you."

Matt gazed at Chad's face, noticeably impressed. He hadn't really gotten a good look at him at the party at Lenora's that night. At least Carson lived up to that part of his bargain.

A lot had been changed. His hair color was different, his nose had been trimmed down, even the basic structure of his face had been skillfully, professionally altered. But there were some things even surgery couldn't change, like his eyes, and his lifelong penchant for sweets.

Kate had done some good detective work to figure this out. He was angry with her for taking the chances that had put her there in the first place, but he was also quite proud of her. At the moment, though, he was more concerned with getting her to safety. Congratulations could come later.

"Okay, Chad," Matt said seriously, keeping his voice down and moving his head constantly to keep an eye on both ends of the corridor. "I want you to go from cell to cell just in case. If there are any other prisoners, Carson might decide to get rid of them once we've escaped. You'll all have to answer to the law, but maybe they'll listen to you and decide being alive in prison is better than being dead or whatever else Carson has planned for you."

Chad took a deep breath and blew it out. "Yeah. I can speak with the voice of experience, all right."

"Don't waste any time. If there are any others and they aren't with us, they're against us. Just leave them locked up and move on. Kate and I will wait for you at the end of the corridor near the stairs." He pointed. "Got it?"

"Got it."

While Chad went about his task, Kate and Matt went down the long, narrow hallway, stopping just before it turned sharply to the right at the foot of the stairs. Matt poked his head around, saw no one, and turned back to Kate. Chad was hurrying down the corridor toward them, frowning.

"All the cells are empty," Chad informed

them, "except the one on the far end. I think you'd better come look."

"Stay here, Kate. If you hear anyone coming down the stairs, give a whistle and come running."

"All right," she replied, trying to sound brave though her knees were shaking. "Shouldn't I have a gun?"

Matt frowned. "Do you know how to use one?"

"No."

"Then it would be safer if you didn't." He threw both pistols into one of the locked cells. "There. I don't carry one either. I've found that if you do, people tend to shoot first and ask questions later. We might get caught, but at least we'll be alive to try again."

He and Chad went to the opposite end of the hall. In the last cell a man sat on the bed smoking a cigarette, his back leaning against the concrete wall. He looked up when Matt's face appeared at the small opening in the door.

"You!" Matt exclaimed.

The man nodded slowly, his expression one of bitter resignation. "The name is Angelo, Mr. Gage. I figured it would not be long before you showed up. You are a slippery one."

"And you are a terrible driver," Matt shot back. "Did you enjoy your swim the other day?"

Angelo shrugged. "The water was warm. Carson's reception for me when I told him I had failed to kill you yet again was even warmer, however." He smiled wryly, stood up, and came over to the door. "Carson frowns upon failure. I have become an embarrassment to him. I don't suppose I could persuade you to let me out before he feeds me to the sharks?"

"And have you whack me on the head the moment my back is turned?" Matt laughed derisively. "I don't think so, friend."

"That would accomplish nothing. They would recapture you and I would still be fed to the fish. I am a proud man, Gage," Angelo said seriously. "Carson has taken my honor from me. I will kill him for what he has done to me, even if I die in the attempt." He grimaced, then added with a wicked grin, "I can help you. You will not escape without that help."

Matt looked at him through the tiny barred opening. He was probably as bad as they came, but there was a certain logic in what he was saying. Carson wasn't the type of man who granted reprieves. It would make him seem weak, and his strength was the only thing that kept his group of killers in awe of him. No wonder Angelo had turned on him.

"I'm listening," Matt said quietly.

"I know the island. I know where the guards patrol. I can show you a way to get out of this part of the house without getting caught." He smiled at the thoughtful expression on Matt's face. "And I also know how to get my hands on something I think you would like to have."

"What?"

"A computer disc with all the names and locations of Carson's clients, with bank account numbers and details of their new identities. That would be helpful, yes?"

Matt nodded. "Yes. Tell me where."

"You do not trust me?" Angelo chuckled. "I do not trust you, either. Let me out and I will show you."

"Leave him," Chad said.

"No." Matt sighed. "He's right. We need help." He put the key in the lock, turned it, then put his hand on Angelo's shoulder as soon as the man stepped out of the cell. "One false move and I'll tear you apart. Understand?"

Angelo nodded. "Yes. But you will not regret this."

"I'd better not, or you most definitely will," Matt returned in a voice full of quiet threat. "Now, how do we get out of here?"

"This way."

He led them back up the corridor to where Kate stood guarding the stairs. Her eyes widened in shock when she saw the new addition to the group.

"What on earth is he doing here?"

"It's a long story," Matt told her. "Angelo says he's going to help us, and I believe him. For the moment."

Angelo bowed slightly to her. "We must hurry. They will come looking for the guards soon. That cell," he said, pointing across the hall, "is not a cell at all, but the entrance to a passageway leading to the beach."

"It doesn't come out anywhere near the aircraft landing strip by any chance?" Matt asked.

"It does."

Chad shook his head. "It's a good thought, Matt, but there isn't much fuel left in my plane."

"You can refuel it," Angelo assured him. "The truck is nearby, and no one guards it at night."

"How about the runway itself?"

Angelo nodded. "One man. Leave him to me."

The cell looked like all the others, but a cleverly disguised door in one wall swung open when Angelo touched the correct spot, revealing a dank, dimly lighted passageway. Trying not to think about what creatures might be living there, Kate followed Matt and Angelo into it, with Chad bringing up the rear. The hidden door swung shut behind them, and the foursome forged ahead into the gloom.

At first the floor was dry, but as they hurried on they began to splash through pools of muddy water, evidence of the nearby ocean. Finally, with a collective, quiet sigh of relief, they emerged into the thick vegetation near the airstrip. In a clearing before them, Chad's plane glistened in the moonlight, its wings dripping water from a recent tropical shower. The ground was soggy beneath their feet.

Angelo motioned for them to be quiet and stay down. Then, before Matt could grab him, he disappeared silently into the dark, junglelike growth. Tension-filled moments passed, and they wondered if they had been abandoned.

But a muffled cry from somewhere out on the runway interrupted their thoughts, and Angelo came back grinning from ear to ear. "I have begun to repay my debt," he whispered. "Your path is now clear, at least until you start the plane. After that . . ." He shrugged.

"The fuel truck?" Matt asked.

"Over there. Its hose should reach the plane."

"Good." Matt turned to Kate and Chad. "Angelo and I have some business to attend to back at the house. You two gas up the plane and get ready to take off. We'll be back."

"What are you going to do?" Kate demanded.

"Get Carson's client list if I can without too much risk. Angelo is going to show me where it is."

But when he turned to look at him, it was obvious Angelo's plans had changed. In his hand was a gun he had taken from the guard he had subdued, and it was pointed at Matt.

"That will not be necessary," Angelo said.

Matt shook his head, disgusted with himself. "What now? Are you going to try to make a deal with your boss?"

"You are mistaken, Gage. This is not to stop you from leaving," he replied. "This is to stop you from trying to take me with you. I have had a taste of being locked up, and I do not like it. But don't worry. I will live up to my bargain." He reached inside his shirt, withdrew a computer disc, and handed it carefully to Matt. "Carson's guards are lazy. They did not search me thoroughly. On that disc is all the information I told you about."

Matt looked at the disc, then at Angelo.

"When we get back to the Caymans, we'll notify the authorities. You'll be caught anyway."

"I doubt it," he said with an odd, resigned smile. "I told you that I am a proud man, Gage. Carson must die. He keeps a great deal of explosives here, to help blow up evidence at accident sites and such. Ammunition too, for the soldiers and his gunboat. It will be quite spectacular when I take a match to it all."

"You'll be killed too," Matt said.

Angelo shrugged. "It is better than prison. And one never knows." His smile faded as he turned to Kate. "I am sorry for your husband. If it matters, I have never killed anyone in my life. But I am sorry for a great many things. When you are in the air, perhaps you will see my attempt to repay those debts as well."

With that he bowed slightly and backed away from the group, said something in Spanish, then turned and disappeared quietly into the darkness before Matt could stop him.

"Damn! Let's get that plane fueled and get out of here. I don't want to be around if he manages to complete his plans."

The trio rushed out onto the landing strip and found the fuel truck. Matt began unreeling a hose from it to the wing of Chad's plane. "We can't risk the noise of starting the truck. I guess we'll have to pump it by hand."

"That'll take some time," Chad informed him.

"Time we don't have," Matt agreed. "We'll just have to get as much in as we can. Things are going to start jumping around here pretty soon."

As they started to fill the plane's tanks manually, however, the staccato sound of gunfire suddenly broke the silence, coming from the direction of the escarpment on the other side of the island. They looked at one another for a moment. Somebody had discovered Angelo.

"Forget it," Matt said. "Start the truck and get the pump going. Let's just hope he keeps them busy for a while." He looked at Kate. "What was that he said just before he took off?"

"I don't think he plans on getting out of here before the explosives go up, Matt," she replied quietly. "He asked God to have mercy on his soul."

Chad was getting edgy. "That's a lot of shooting for just one man," he said, looking uneasily around the clearing. "What's going on?"

"Maybe Angelo has friends, or somehow managed to get them all shooting at each other," Matt replied. "Either way, I think we'd better get going right now. How's the fuel?"

Chad checked the gauge. "Maybe."

"It'll have to do."

The trio wasted no time in piling into the plane. Chad pushed the twin-engined aircraft to its limit and they went bouncing down the rough, soggy runway, easing into the air with scant inches to spare above the treetops. As they climbed steeply into the darkness, Kate grabbed Matt's hand for reassurance.

"Easy, Kate. Those are the only fingers I've got," he said, easing her grip and putting an arm around her. "Nice takeoff, Chad."

"Thanks." He banked the plane left, and they all looked out the side windows at the dark shape of the island below. "Boy, something's going on down there. Look's like a war zone."

From their vantage point high above Carson's private island the three could see a pitched battle taking place on the ground below. Even with a full moon it was still too dark to make out details, but judging from the widely scattered flashes of light there was a lot of gunfire. Here and there beams of flashlights bounced and waved as the men carrying them ran around looking for something.

"It looks as though Carson's men have divided into groups and are fighting each other," Matt said. "Someone must have spotted Angelo going into the munitions dump, made the connection, and decided to leave. The others are trying to stop them."

"I hope he succeeds," Chad said bitterly.

"Me too," Kate agreed.

"Make it unanimous," Matt said. "But you didn't hear me say that. I'm supposed to say that Carson should be brought to justice."

Chad uttered a short, curt laugh. "If Angelo makes it, he will be. Or at least the kind of justice he deserves."

"How about us, Chad?" Matt asked. "Will we make it?"

"We should. The fuel level looks pretty good." He held a bag of lollipops out to them. "Want some candy?"

"No thanks," they replied at the same time.

Kate looked at Matt, managing a shaky smile. "I'm glad we got out in one piece. And right now, I don't care where we go. Any place where Carson isn't will be fine with me." She kissed him on the cheek. "And as long as we're together."

"I know this is a strange time to ask," Matt said, gazing at her tenderly, "but when we get back, will you . . ." His voice trailed off as something caught his attention. He pointed at the dark spot of land below. "Look."

On the craggy cliff where Carson's circular house stood, long tongues of flame had begun to shoot into the air. Deep in the bowels of the cliff, Angelo had done his work. A series of small explosions shattered the rock, hurling pieces into the sea.

Then a much larger explosion came, a blast so powerful the three in the plane could feel the buffeting wind of the shock wave rocking the plane as they flew away. Rocks, palm trees and other shattered debris went soaring into the air. Part of the seething fireball broke off and the flaming, splintered remnants of Carson's house tumbled from the clifftop into the sea.

"Good Lord! The whole island's on fire," Chad said in an awestruck voice. "They're all goners."

"Couldn't happen to a nicer group," Matt agreed.

Kate stared at the inferno disappearing behind them. "Is he . . ." She stopped, afraid to even ask.

"It's all over," Matt assured her. "They won't

find enough left of Carson to sweep into a dustpan."

She shuddered and closed her eyes, leaning against him, sighing as his arms closed protectively around her. There was an odd feeling inside her, relief of course, but something else. She struggled to identify it, at last recognizing it as a feeling of having been cheated in some way. Carson was dead. Why should vengeance still burn within her?

"It's over," she told herself firmly, repeating the words as she drifted into an exhausted sleep in Matt's strong arms. "It's over."

Matt strolled down the powdery ribbon of West Bay Beach, enjoying the soothing Caymanian sunshine and the way the waves lapped at his bare feet. The tension of the last several days was at an end. Kate was safe, Carson's empire was crumbling, and all those who deserved it were either already behind bars or soon would be.

It was a pleasant thought to know that Lenora was in police custody, especially since it looked like Chad would receive a lighter sentence than his wife for all the help he had given them. When Matt had called Stacy Burch to let her know what had happened, she had laughed, told him to thank Kate for her advice, then had said goodbye quickly so she wouldn't be late for a date with her new boyfriend—a very handsome veterinarian who was, as Stacy put it, very well off and on the verge of proposing.

Matt watched as Kate bounded out of the surf,

shrieking happily, salt spray cascading around her. Water droplets glistened on her smooth, tanned skin, the sight of her lithe form in the bikini she wore making him almost dizzy with longing and anticipation.

She stopped to pick her towel off the sand, deliberately teasing him as she did so, knowing how her breasts were displayed by the skimpy top when she bent over. Then she walked toward him, dragging the end of the towel along the beach instead of wrapping it around her. Her eyes twinkled with mischief.

"You'll pay," he assured her, his voice full of sensual threat.

"Promise?"

He pulled her into his arms, heedless of the way her damp body soaked his slacks and crisp white shirt. "Yes. And you know I always keep my promises."

They kissed, barely keeping their passion in check, then linked arms and strolled back toward their bungalow, the need to leave the public beach sudden and overwhelming.

"How did your meeting with Dale go?" she asked.

"He's enjoying his impromptu and tax-deductible stay in the Caymans. And I got paid," he answered simply.

Kate chuckled. "I knew you had a mercenary streak."

"More than you know. I only turned over a partial list of Carson's clients to him, just the ones who had defrauded Fidelity. I'll deal with the other insurance companies myself."

"You're terrible!"

"Never said I wasn't," he agreed amiably. She tried to get away from him, but he put his arm around her waist and held her tight. "I have to look out for my own business interests. Why let Dale get all the glory?"

Kate looked at him, feigning shock, but couldn't keep it up for long. "You're right. We're the ones who deserve the credit. We did all the work and took all the risks. He just paid the expenses."

"We?"

She bit him playfully on the arm. "Say it."

"Ouch! All right." He looked into her eyes, suddenly serious. "I couldn't have done it without you, Kate. Is that what you want to hear?"

"Some of it," she replied, poking him in the ribs. "A word or two of thanks would be nice too."

"For what?"

"You beast!"

Matt swept her into his arms and carried her onto the bungalow's private patio, Kate flailing her arms and legs all the way. He put her down in a padded chaise and held her there as she struggled, cutting off her heated protests by covering her mouth with his own. His tongue dove between her parted lips, devouring her, until her insulted cries turned into moans of pleasure.

"Thank you," he murmured softly against the skin of her neck. "Thank you for helping me, and for being every bit the stubborn, impetuous, eager—"

"Shut up and kiss me again," she interrupted. "You can thank me some more later."

He did, then pulled up a chair and sat beside her, content for the moment to simply look at her. Kate returned his gaze through half-lidded eyes, enjoying the feeling of just being near him.

"Did you tell Dale how helpful I was?" she asked.

"I did." He laughed. "He was quite chagrined. I think you'll be receiving an apology from him soon. Once he gets over the fit of apoplexy he had when he saw my expense account, that is."

Kate laughed with him. Then her smile slowly waned. "Did they find Carson's . . ."

"From all eyewitness accounts by the survivors who were rescued from the island, both Angelo and Carson were right on top of the explosives when they went off."

"They could be lying."

Matt shook his head. "They had no reason to. Except for an elite, rabid core, they hated Carson to a man. He held them together with a web of money and fear, not the kind of regime designed to make for loyal followers," he told her. "His empire was falling apart already. He could no longer control all the pieces. He'd pushed his clients too far, his men even farther, and when they saw it toppling they all raced to give it a push."

"Still . . ."

"He's dead, Kate. It really is over."

She sat up and hugged him. "I keep telling myself that. It just seems so inconclusive, that's all. Like the accidents he arranged. No body, just enough proof to satisfy the authorities."

"Very perceptive, Mrs. Asher."

The hair on the back of Kate's neck stood up at the sound of the cold, brittle voice that came from the bungalow doorway. Matt spun in his chair, already halfway to his feet.

"Sit down, Mr. Gage," Carson commanded casually. The large-caliber automatic he held in his hand glinted in the sunlight. "Your time will come soon enough. Let's not rush it. You wouldn't want to spoil my enjoyment, would you?"

Kate felt fear and rage mingle within her, making her stomach tighten painfully. "No," she whispered. "It can't be. You're dead."

"Not quite." Carson stepped out of the shadow of the doorway, his horrible smile half hidden by bandages on one side of his face. "Although I must admit, Angelo made a valiant attempt. If he had shown that much initiative in getting rid of you two, none of this would have happened in the first place." His shrug made him wince. "You've caused me considerable annoyance, Gage. As you were so compassionately assuring the young lady, I have lost everything."

"Not quite everything," Matt ground out through clenched teeth. "You're still alive. But not to worry. I'll take over where Angelo left off."

"No false heroics, please," Carson said, moving the gun to point it at Kate. "I assure you I'll pull the trigger. As I said, I've precious little left to lose. My island is gone, my network is being methodically and thoroughly destroyed as we speak, and all of my funds—save a paltry million or so in a Swiss account—have been either impounded or are now beyond my reach because my puppets are in jail."

Kate glared at the man in the shadows, anger boiling within her. It was impossible for him to still be alive, but he was. Maybe he was just too evil to die. But the reverse was true as well. He was too evil to live. It was not enough to send him to prison. The more she thought about it, the more her hatred grew, her hidden dreams of revenge once again bubbling to the surface.

"But I can build again," Carson said, continuing his gloating, psychotic speech. "Hand over the disc Angelo stole."

"Not while I'm still breathing," Matt bit out. Every muscle in his body seemed coiled, like a steel spring ready to lash out viciously. "You won't walk away this time, Carson."

Carson laughed. "I'm going to enjoy this, Gage," he said as he leveled the big handgun at him.

"Damn you!" As if in a dream, Kate felt her legs tense, realized that she was getting out of her chair. It couldn't be her who turned to face Carson, but it was, and her eyes were full of hatred. "You should be dead!"

It was such a totally unexpected move that Carson paused and turned to look curiously at the madwoman daring to confront him. Matt didn't wait for him to regain his composure. He launched himself at Carson headfirst, his full weight and the massive power of his legs driving into the other man as he hit him in the stomach with his shoulder.

The air left Carson's lungs in a harsh gasp and he tumbled back into the living room, Matt right on top of him. The gun went flying through the air and landed with a metallic clatter on the patio at Kate's feet. She stared at it, still feeling as if a part of her was observing the whole scene from somewhere else.

Miraculously, Carson managed to squirm out from under Matt, gasping for breath and holding his ribs. Matt got to his hands and knees, a bit dazed from the force of the blow himself. Carson staggered forward, then stopped at the patio door, his eyes wide with surprise.

Kate stood before him, the gun clenched in both hands. She pointed it at her tormentor, her heartbeat seeming unnaturally loud in her ears. She barely heard the voice that spoke to her, only part of her realizing it was Matt and that he was saying something important.

"Don't do it, Kate. He's done for already."

"He has to die." Was that her voice?

"The law will handle him, Kate," Matt said, moving toward her. Carson weaved unsteadily in the doorway, blocking Matt's exit and putting him in Kate's line of fire. "Be careful with that thing!" he exclaimed. "Give it to me."

"No." Had she said that? The gun was very heavy. It waved in front of her as she pointed it at

Carson, her finger curled around the trigger. "I can't."

Matt looked at her, fear knotting his stomach. Her hatred for Carson had taken over, and though he couldn't blame her at all, he had to get her to listen. If she fired the gun, she could very well hit him instead of Carson. And Carson was growing more unsteady by the moment. If he made a lunge for her there was no telling what might happen. She might be killed herself.

"Why are you doing this, Kate?"

The gun steadied. "For Paul," she said in a voice cracked with emotion. "For Gloria's husband and her little baby boy."

"No, you're not. You're doing it for yourself," he told her desperately. "This has been for you all along, hasn't it? Were you just using me, Kate? Did you get close to me, make me fall in love with you, all so you could do this?"

"No!" She looked at Matt. "How can you say that?"

"I'm saying it because I love you, Kate. Do you love me?" he asked her.

Kate's vision blurred with tears. "You know I do."

"No, I don't. Tell me."

"I love you."

"And I love you. Don't do this, Kate. It's murder. He deserves it, I know, but this isn't the way."

"Prison? No. He has to die."

"Dammit, Kate! Listen to me. Think about our future. It will be full of growth and sharing, sweeter by far than any revenge. The past is bitter, Kate. Let it go."

Tears rolled down her cheeks. "Paul . . ."

"Paul is gone, Kate. So is David Tynly. You can't bring them back. Gloria and her baby will go on with their lives and so will we. Together. You and I and a family of our own."

She started to weep openly and lowered the gun, then let it slip from her trembling hands. Matt stepped over Carson as he fell to his knees in the doorway and kicked it out of reach.

He wrapped Kate in his arms, holding her as she sobbed the remnants of her past away against his broad chest. The dark, hidden dream of vengeance she had carried for so long was draining out of her, replaced by the light of her love for Matt, by the love she could feel within him as well.

"I love you, Matt. I love you so much!"

"And I love you, Kate. With all my heart."

"You should have let her shoot me, Gage," Carson wheezed as he pushed himself up to a standing position. "At last, you have made a mistake." He pulled a smaller revolver out of his coat pocket, lifted it, and squeezed the trigger.

A loud report split the air. But Carson's gun dangled from his finger, unfired. Kate and Matt watched in shocked confusion as he slowly toppled forward, falling on his face on the stone patio, dead this time beyond a shadow of a doubt.

The man with the gun behind them had seen to it, as he had vowed he would. "Good-bye, Carson," Angelo said.

Kate's mouth was too dry for her to speak. Matt managed to mumble "How did you . . ."

"I have arranged a great many accidents," Angelo replied. "Unfortunately, they have all been designed to make people look like they have died when actually they have survived. What can I say?" he shrugged. "I guess I got too good at them. Now, if you will excuse me, I think I'll go pretend to be dead somewhere. *Adios!*"

"He's getting away, Matt."

Matt nodded, but merely hugged her, then led her back down to the beach and away from the bungalow. "I know. Let someone else go after him," he said. "I've had more than enough justice for quite some time. Right now, all I want is you."

"Only right now?" Kate asked, her heart free at last.

"Forever," Matt replied. "And that's a promise."

CHAPTER SIXTEEN

"Hi, gorgeous," Matt murmured, gazing down at the woman slowly awakening in his arms.

Kate stretched sensuously, rubbing her smooth legs against his hairy ones as she nuzzled closer to him.

Matt laughed softly, hugging her tight. "Are you hungry?"

Her eyes popped opened immediately. "What did you have in mind?" she asked saucily, raking her fingernails down his chest to his taut stomach.

"Food, you witch! Sustenance to help me keep up with your insatiable appetites."

"My appetites?" Kate grabbed a pillow and proceeded to whack him with it, only causing him to laugh uproariously at her outrage. Finally she stopped and fell on top of him.

"Oof!" he gasped as she hit his empty stomach. "You're smothering me."

"I haven't even begun," she threatened.

"Enough, you heartless wench, I can't fight back when I'm weak with hunger."

"I know," she purred, launching herself at him again.

Matt grabbed hold of her flying hands and held them loosely together with one of his. "Control yourself. You can have all of me you want later."

"Promises, promises," she taunted before rolling away from him. "Last one in the kitchen has to cook," she yelled, already on her way.

She was relaxing at the breakfast nook table when he wandered into the room. "Lost your way?" she asked.

He had put on a pair of jeans and a pullover top. "I know when I'm beat. Now scram while I fix breakfast, or I'll eat you instead."

He advanced toward her, licking his lips. The chartreuse nightshirt she wore left her arms and legs partially bare, not to mention the dipping neckline that taunted him with a view of her soft breasts.

"Cook!" she demanded, sidestepping his grasp.

Kate breezed through a shower and applied her makeup with a light hand, then looked closely in the mirror while she dressed. It was shocking how much of an improvement could be made with a little help from the cosmetic companies. Navy blue shorts and a striped top completed her outfit, and she was ready to do battle.

And a battle was exactly what she expected. The past month had been glorious, full of blissful days and nights, a honeymoon more perfect than Kate had dreamed possible. But she was determined to be Matt's partner in everything, not just matrimony, and didn't doubt for a moment that her demands would cause their first real argument as a married couple.

Then there was the little surprise she had for him. It would cause quite an uproar too. Matt wasn't going to like it that she had accepted a job for them without consulting him, but then she wasn't exactly thrilled with him right now, either, after what he had pulled the day before.

"I'm starting without you," Matt yelled.

She waltzed into the kitchen and sat down, taking a bite of her breakfast. "Mmm," Kate mumbled. "Great waffles."

Sonja had been watching her anxiously. She put her cold nose on Kate's thigh and tried to look pitiful. Kate slipped her a bit of waffle.

"Hey!" Matt cried. "Don't feed Sonja those! They aren't good for her digestion."

Two pairs of innocent eyes looked up at him. "But she loves them."

"That's beside the point."

Her waffle was all gone anyway. "Okay," she agreed, letting Sonja lick her fingers clean of syrup.

"What am I going to do with you?" he asked with a long-suffering sigh.

She smiled at him. "Make me your partner, remember?" she returned. "When do we start our next exciting case?"

Matt pursed his lips and held up his left hand, wiggling his fingers to indicate his wedding ring. "I've already made you my partner."

"I'm not talking about that," she said, glaring at him. "And I don't mean doing your filing and stamp licking either. When do I get to the really good part?"

"Never."

"You're not taking on anymore interesting cases?"

"I am, *you* are not. Besides, isn't it time for you to be back in school?"

She looked around the kitchen vaguely. "No."

"Kathryn!"

"Yes, love?" she asked sweetly.

"Are you listening to me?"

"Don't I always?"

Matt laughed. "Do you ever? And you don't fool me for a minute with that innocent routine."

"I remember you telling me the cases you took weren't dangerous," she said, pouting.

"They usually aren't."

"Well, then. There isn't any reason why I can't help with investigations, question witnesses—"

"No."

Kate sat there for a moment, stroking Sonja, obviously lost in thought. Then she got up and began cleaning up the kitchen, Matt warily helping her load the dishwasher.

"What are you thinking now?" Truthfully, he was almost afraid to find out. He could practically hear the gears grinding away in her brain.

"I think our working together should be open to negotiation," she announced calmly, leading the way into the living room. "You did admit that I was a big help on the last assignment."

"Under duress." Matt sighed loudly. She wasn't going to give up. Her taste for adventure had been ignited and now she wanted more fuel to fan the flames. "And you have been a big help to me the last few days."

"If you mean that deadly boring stuff you gave me to do yesterday," she said disdainfully, patting the couch and watching as Sonja jumped up beside her, "you can think again. I'm talking a serious partnership here. Like last time."

"Kate!" He would strangle her yet. "Not only are you trying to turn my world upside down, but you are also spoiling an excellent guard dog!"

"I am not." She looked into Sonja's eyes and pointed at Matt. "Sic 'em!" Sonja yawned and put her big head in Kate's lap.

"She knows which side her bread is buttered on," Matt said, settling himself comfortably in an overstuffed chair across from her. This was going to take a while.

"Meaning that I don't, I suppose?"

"I didn't say that," he returned calmly. "But you do have to realize that you can't go jumping into these things. I'm trying to teach you to be methodical and patient and—"

"You mean you bored me to tears on purpose?" she accused, getting up and pacing around the large, airy living room, more than ready to vent her anger.

"Yes," he replied, not in the least put out by her observation. Her auburn hair definitely was showing more of a tendency toward bright red, with the fiery temper to go with it. "You have to start somewhere."

Sonja paced back and forth with her, and when

Kate stopped in front of him, hands on her hips, she gazed balefully at him as well.

Matt rubbed his face with his hands. "Ye gods! You've even got the dog on your side."

"She knows I'm right." Blue eyes flashing, Kate glared at him, the jerk of her head sending her hair flying. "I know you normally don't take on such boring work yourself."

He took a sip of his tea. "It was a routine case."

"And you take those all the time?" she asked, sarcasm dripping from her voice.

"They do pay the bills."

"You don't fool me for a minute, Matthew. I had a very interesting and long talk with Rita yesterday afternoon."

He smiled. She had gotten a lot further than he thought she would. "Then you did finish the file?"

"Yes, and I also know she or someone else usually deals with all that dried up, tedious research."

He laughed openly now. "True."

"Well, you can wipe that silly grin off your face. Tomorrow won't be nearly as boring," she informed him, boldly taking a drink of his tea.

Matt sat up straighter at her announcement. "What have you done now?"

Kate waved her hand vaguely. "Oh, nothing much."

"Kathryn!"

"Some insurance company I've never heard of wants you to look into the disappearance of

. . ." She paused, enjoying herself for a moment. His thunderous expression made her decide to go on. "Jewels," she completed dramatically.

"No!"

"Too late, I assured them you'd take the case." Kate set his cup down and began to back away as Matt stood up. She didn't like the expression on his face. "I checked your files to verify that you'd worked for them previously," she assured him, "before I agreed."

"How considerate of you!" he bellowed, coming after her as she backed away from him. Sonja joined him, enjoying this new game.

The pair continued to stalk Kate across the room, and she took off running into their at-home office. "Now, Matt, calm down," she ordered from behind the safety of his desk.

He didn't say a word, just kept coming toward her. She glanced around the room, unsure of where to run next. That slight hesitation was her undoing. Sonja came around the other side of the desk, growling playfully.

"Matthew," she yelped as he grabbed her and swung her up over his shoulder. "What are you doing?" She was hanging upside down staring at his back as he strolled out of the office and toward the bedroom.

"Pipe down," he ordered.

"Sonja!" Kate cried. "Help me!"

But Sonja had seen this game before, and wasn't particularly interested. She almost seemed to shrug at the folly of humans, and went to see if there were any waffles left.

Matt chuckled evilly. "Now she knows I'm right. I'm doing the only logical thing."

"What?"

"I'm going to tie you up, for your own safety," he informed her, opening the bedroom door.

"Don't you dare," she yelled, struggling in earnest now.

He casually dropped her on the bed and watched her bounce gently on the soft covers. "What am I going to do with you, Kate?"

"Keep me," she whispered huskily, holding her arms out to him.

Matt leaned over her, letting her wrap her arms around his neck and pull him down on top of her. "You'll never get away," he said, wrapping her tightly in his embrace.

"I don't want to. I'm here to stay." She peeked at him through half-closed eyes. "You'll take the case?" He sighed and nodded his surrender. "You'll make me a full-fledged partner, let me investigate right alongside you?"

"Do I have a choice?"

"No."

He sighed again. "Then I guess I'll have to keep you."

"Because you couldn't do it without me?"

"No," he replied. "Because I would never want to." Rolling over, he took her with him on a ride that would never end. They belonged together, and Kate intended to make this dream last forever.